WEIRD WILD

WEIRD WILD
Geraldine Clark Hellery

www.foxspirit.co.uk

Weird Wild Copyright © 2014 by Geraldine Clark Hellery

Cover and Internal Art by Matthew Clark Hellery

typesetting and conversion by handebooks.co.uk

ISBN: 978-1-909348-41-7 epub
ISBN: 978-1-909348-42-4 mobi
ISBN: 978-1-909348-43-1 paperback

All rights reserved, including the right to reproduce this book or portions thereof in any form.

A Fox Spirit Original
Fox Spirit Books
www.foxspirit.co.uk
adele@foxspirit.co.uk

To my husband, Matthew, and Bob. All my love. Forever.

Contents

Introduction to 'Weird Wild'	9
The Camp Site	11
The Lake	25
The Dragon Tree	33
The Bridge	36
The Mountain	42
The Stone Circle	46
The Cairn	65
The Swamp	69
The Lookout Point	71
The Bluebell Wood	89
The Teddy Bears' Picnic	91
Back to the Campsite	99

Introduction to 'Weird Wild'

Well firstly a big thank you for picking up my little tome, my first collection of short stories, and poems. It's been a long trip to publication for these stories with them written over a period of personal ups and downs.

'Weird Wild' has always been a challenge: the first story I wrote was 'The Lake' as part of an online writing course where participants had to write a short story describing the main character through their environment. I immediately saw a man stood looking out over a beautiful lake: the setting was majestic but the intent was evil. I remember writing it just before moving to a new city and reading it to my new writers group. When I finished there was the sort of stunned silence you normally only get on reality TV before the judges offer their pronouncement before the thoughtful judgement 'We like it'.

I put 'The Lake' aside and wrote other stories, short and long when something sparked what was to become 'Back to the Campsite'. Again I wanted to challenge my writing so it's all in the first person and trying to redefine an age old myth. After that I decided to create an entire forest's worth of stories in a mixture of styles and genres and to push myself in areas I wouldn't consider my forte, such as poetry (yes, two poems made it into the final selection and I'm really pleased with how they turned out). I have also included a slightly amended version of 'Into the Woods' which was my first ever published short story (first published in 'Tales of the Nun and Dragon' from Fox Spirit Books).

While 'Weird Wild' has been a writing challenge, it's also been a personal one as well. In June 2013 I suffered a series of losses and in order to drag myself through the fog of grief and depression I set myself the challenge of finishing a cohesive and interlinked set of short stories and poems. It was just what I needed and I was honoured when the amazing Adele Wearing, owner of Fox Spirit Books, agreed to publish these stories and my husband agreed to design the cover and beautiful internal drawings.

The stories collated here in 'Weird Wild' are set in the fictional woods of Foundry Forest, located somewhere in the UK but all are inspired in some part by the tales and myths from all regions of the UK and further afield. Walking amongst our beautiful countryside you might recognise the setting of the 'Stone Circle', or see the trolls living under 'The Bridge'. Have a swim in 'The Lake' before settling down for toasted marshmallows at 'The Campsite'. Be careful in spring when the sound of bells can be heard in 'The Bluebell Wood' and never trust a bear if they invite you for a picnic. So come along, take a walk with me through the Weird Wild Woods. Just pack a picnic. And a knife.

The Camp Site

'Eeew, Dad, there's a man on the other side of the lake and there's a floating woman that he's pushing like a boat,' yelled Peter.

George looked up from the tent poles in his hands. 'What are you talking about, Peter?'

'He's killed a woman and now he's trying to drown her in the lake,' called Peter's brother Carl as he joined his brother on the lake shore.

'Camp side stories,' chuckled George as he looked at his wife Lucy who giggled into her book.

'Boys, come over here and give me a hand with this tent,' said George as he studied the instructions intently. Finally he threw the instructions aside in disgust. His sons remained transfixed by the lake. 'It seems like you need a damned PhD to put the stupid thing up,'

'Now, George, remember this was your idea, get outside and enjoy the great outdoors, you said. You should be happy the boys left their video games at home,' chided Lucy as she carefully folded the corner of her page, put her book in her backpack before turning to help her husband lay out the tent canvas and poles. 'You filled the boys' heads with tales of fishing, sleeping under the stars and stories around the campfire. None of us expected soggy leaves, a droopy tent and this damned fog.' Lucy looked up at the trees. A light fog had been dancing around their tips for most of the day but luckily it hadn't sunk down to the forest floor.

'I used to camp all the time as a kid. I didn't remember all the time it took my dad to put up the tent, it was just done in time for toasted marshmallows and ghost stores,' said George.

'And I'm sure our boys will forget all your hard work and only remember the fantastic trip their dad so carefully planned,' smiled Lucy warmly, 'Now get out of the way, you're putting it up inside out. Go take the boys for a walk through the woods or something while I sort the tent out.'

George humphed and looked as if he was about to say

more but then he saw the firm set of his wife's lips and knew further arguing was useless. And in his heart he knew she would put the tent up in half the time it would take him, without breaking a sweat and more importantly, without breaking the tent. Following instructions wasn't his strong point.

He silently handed his wife the tent pole and nodded his agreement, 'Come on boys, we're going for a walk while your mum sorts out the tents.'

The boys dragged themselves away from what they had been watching on the lake.

'But dad, the man,' started Peter.

'Let's go boys, or your mum will get us to peel the potatoes for dinner,' replied George. The threat of cooking drove the children to their father's side and they happily ran in the direction he pointed them in as he picked up his walking stick and slowly started following their happy squeals.

'And George, don't let them eat any of the berries, a lot of them are poisonous if you don't know what you are eating,' called Lucy, the tent already taking shape with efficient snaps. George did not turn around but merely acknowledged his wife's comment with a wave of his hand and a roll of his eyes.

The boys pushed each other good-naturedly as Carl called out, 'Tell us another one.'

Lucy smiled lovingly at her sons, so full of life and energy. They had returned from their walk with tales of misshapen trees, strange animal noises and lots of unidentifiable plants their father had forbidden them from touching. George had simply shrugged in answer to Lucy's questioning look.

'Mum, when we get home, can I join the scouts? I want to learn all about the forest and how to live here and go camping and learn how to use a penknife and learn about what plants I can eat and I want to only eat food cooked on a bar-be-que and, and, and,' Peter looked concerned for a moment as he searched for additional things he might learn in the scouts.

'Mum, I want to join the scouts too,' Carl chimed in.

'They wouldn't let a wimp like you join the scouts,' teased Peter. Carl's anger rose and he started to push his brother.

'Boys, go wash your hands, dinner's nearly ready,' Lucy said in a firm voice before the boys could start their usual over-zealous play fighting. 'Carl, pump the water for your brother and boys, don't take too long, I'm serving up now.'

The two brothers walked across the small clearing where their mother had set up a small container with a hand-pump to pump the water, still pushing and teasing each other.

Lucy looked at George who was watching his sons with a proud expression.

'So I take it the walk was a success then?' she asked.

George turned to his wife with a broad grin. 'They loved it! They were into everything, investigating rabbit holes, sticking their fingers in dead trees, jumping over brooks. It's like they were born to be out here.'

Lucy laughed at the idea of her two sons who usually stayed sat in front of the TV or video games, enjoying playing without the need for a power point or joystick. 'And did you see any wild life? There's supposed to be lots of critters around here.'

George looked thoughtful before he answered, 'Strangely no. I thought we'd see a lot more, even with the Terrible Two hollering around the place like a pair of Tasmanian devils.'

'Wrong country but good description,' Lucy pulled a bottle of beer from the cooler box and popped the bottle top off, handing it to her husband before repeating the process for herself.

'Can I have a beer mum?' asked Peter as he joined his parents wiping his clean hands on his dirty jeans. Lucy started to say something but rolled her eyes instead as Carl copied his brother, wiping his hands on his equally dirty jeans.

'When you're older,' the parents replied in unison.

Peter started to pout but was deftly distracted as Lucy started setting plates on the foldaway table.

After they had finished their meals, the family sat back in their comfy chairs and rubbed their stomachs in satisfaction.

'That was delicious,' Peter burped.

'That was delicious,' Carl copied, also burping. Soon both boys were having an impromptu burping competition, giggling loudly while George looked on indulgently. After a few minutes, Lucy gave the boys a warning look.

Suddenly George slapped his arm. 'Darned mosquitoes,' he muttered.

'Do you know a way to get rid of mosquitoes?' asked Lucy, instantly catching the attention of her boys.

Lucy paused for a moment, momentarily enjoying the peace of the silent concentration of her husband and sons. Just when she knew they would burst with curiosity, she continued, 'Smoke.'

George's eyes lit up in understanding and smiled at his wife.

'I don't understand?' said Peter.

'I don't understand,' mimicked Carl.

'It means we need firewood,' explained Lucy.

'Come on boys, we'll get some wood and we can make a fire and if you ask your mum, she might have marshmallows which need to be toasted,' George heaved himself out of his chair, emitting a loud burp as he did so. Peter and Carl laughed loudly while Lucy rolled her eyes as she began clearing the plates.

'It's times like this I'm so proud of my family,' she muttered as George smiled at her, kissing her quickly on the nose. Hearing their father had set the boys on their burping competition again as they ran into the woods to begin collecting firewood. George grabbed some torches before burping again. He looked sheepishly at his wife as she raised an eyebrow at him. He quickly turned and followed his sons.

'Like father, like son,' muttered Lucy as she set the dirty plates aside and dug out the marshmallows.

'I feel sick,' whined Peter. Soon his younger brother was making vomiting noises.

'Well, I did tell you not to eat so many marshmallows,' replied Lucy, 'But you said you wanted one more. Then one more after that.'

Peter scowled at his logical mother and Lucy suppressed a smile. He looked exactly like his father at times like this.

George interrupted the staring competition his eldest son and wife were having, 'Time for stories,' he said.

'Yeah, ghost stories,' yelled Carl.

'George,' Lucy started in a warning tone.

He waved away her fears.

'Well if they have nightmares, it's all your fault,' said Lucy.

'It'll be fun. We will all take it in turns to tell a story. Who wants to start?' George threw some more twigs on the fire which flared briefly.

The boys looked thoughtful for a moment then shyly pushed back into their chairs. George looked back and forth between his boys for a moment, 'Ok then, I'll start.' He rubbed his chin for a moment before leaning forward, looking intently into the fire and beginning his tale.

George's tale:

'You've heard the stories about Robin Hood, haven't you,' George asked his sons, who nodded in unison, eyes already as big as saucers. 'Well, Robin Hood was not real. But the story was based on a real man. His name was Hidden John.'

'Hidden John?' scoffed Carl.

'Hidden John,' said his father firmly. 'And he lived in these woods.'

'No he didn't. You're just making that up,' said Peter, folding his arms and giving his dad a challenging look which reminded George of Lucy.

He gave his eldest son the same look he gave his wife when she challenged him, 'No son, I'm telling you the truth. His name was Hidden John and he lived here with his band of ruffians and cut-throats.'

'Like pirates?' asked Carl.

George shushed his son before continuing his story.

'Hidden John lived in these parts approximately five hundred years ago. Like in the story of Robin Hood, there was an evil landowner called Sir Moseley who taxed the people to the brink of starvation. Hidden John was a local farmer and Sir Moseley decided he was going to marry Hidden John's eldest daughter. Now, had he allowed the marriage to take place, Hidden John could have expected some help with his taxes as the landowner and he could have fed the rest of his family, but he saw how sad his daughter became. She stopped eating and as the wedding drew nearer, she grew weaker and weaker. Hidden John spoke with Sir Moseley but he refused to cancel the wedding and the night before they were due to get married, Hidden John's daughter killed herself by throwing herself into the lake you see behind you. Hidden John was inconsolable and he blamed Sir Moseley for the problems he had brought on his family. Sir Moseley, deprived of his prize, burned Hidden John's farm down while Hidden John was at the market, selling his crops. Nothing remained and sadly, all Hidden John's family were also killed.'

'What did he do dad?' Peter asked, still saucer-eyed.

'Hidden John decided that Sir Moseley needed to be stopped. So he took whatever tools and weapons that not been burned and he left. He came into the forest. Using his tools he built a simple hut, high up in the trees, where Sir Moseley's men could not find him and at night, he would visit the other farms and houses, telling the people his idea. Soon he had a band of men, and a few women as well, living with him out in the forest. At night, they would raid Sir Moseley's land, killing the animals and setting fire to the crops. They stole from his treasury and distributed his wealth amongst themselves. Sir Moseley became very very angry but try as they might, his men could not find Hidden John or his gang.'

'Cos they were so well hidden in the forest?' Peter interrupted. Carl was hanging on his father's every word.

George shook his head, 'Oh no, they didn't live in the trees anymore because there was too many of them, they moved into the caves. But their secret in their battle against Sir Moseley was that they had found a secret stream. If they drank the water from this stream, it would make them invisible.'

Peter looked unimpressed, 'Invisible?'

Absorbing every word his father said, Carl asked, 'Is that true dad? Was there a magic stream that could make them invisible?'

George struggled to keep the smile from covering his face as he looked at his boys. 'Every word is true boys. We'll go and look for the stream tomorrow and you can drink the water and become invisible.'

'Really dad?' Carl looked around, as if a spring would suddenly appear from one of the trees nearby.

'Course. Now who's next?' said George, spearing another marshmallow and leaning towards the fire.

Carl looked a little uncertain. 'I don't have a story, but we learned a poem at school that the teacher said was about one of the trees in the forest.'

Lucy smiled encouragingly, while Carl scrunched his face in concentration, trying to remember the poem.

Carl's poem:

'I can't remember it all,' he said apologetically.

'Well, just recite what you can remember,' Lucy handed Peter a toasted marshmallow to stop him from distracting his younger brother as Carl started slowly, focussing to remember the poem.

> 'Hopes and seeds were sown,
> Couples danced and sang,
> Their future unknown,
> Their dreams their only plan
> The day the dragon fell to earth.
>
> All the town was there,
> Enjoying the summer sun,
> The villagers were at the fair,

Except the farmer's son,
The day the dragon fell to earth.

The dragon stood tall,
His wings flashed wide,
With his first steps, fall!
He landed at Boys side,
The day the dragon fell to earth.

The dragon's mouth opened wide,
Boy saw the fire burning deep,
As the dragon sighed,
Out his nostrils the fire did seep.
The day the dragon fell to earth.

'Um, then, hang on a second,' Carl scratched his head. 'I can't remember the rest.'

'That's a poem for babies. We learned that last year,' sneered Peter while Lucy shushed him.

'You did very well, Carl. Can you remember what happens at the end?' asked George, ignoring his oldest son.

Carl frowned and his lips puckered a little while he thought. 'Well the boy looks after the dragon and they become friends. But the boy grows old and dies so the dragon can't look after itself any more. Then it gets rained on and dies.'

'Rain kills the dragon?' asked Lucy.

Carl's frown deepened.

Peter sighed dramatically. 'The dragon swallowed the water and it put out the fire in his throat. Cos he didn't have his fire, he died and turned into stone.'

'No he didn't, he turned into a tree,' challenged Carl.

Peter opened his mouth to respond, but Lucy quickly interrupted before the argument could grow. 'Well whatever he turned into, what a poor dragon! Would you like to be a dragon?'

'Yeah, I'd eat all the people and blow fire out of my nose,' yelled Peter excitedly. His younger brother nodded his agreement.

Satisfied she had allayed any potential arguments, Lucy sat back in her fold-up chair. 'Right, now it's my turn.'

'And what is your story about?' asked George.

Lucy smiled wickedly, 'What else would a girl's story be about, but fairies?'

'Nooo,' cried Peter, 'Fairies are for girls,' sulked Peter, crossing his arms.

'Not these fairies,' Lucy said calmly. 'These ones aren't good fairies. They are very naughty and fight with swords and know special magic. But if you think that's too girlie, I'll just tell a different story.'

'Tell us about the naughty fairies,' cried Carl, his excitement rising.

'Well if you're sure,' Lucy feigned nonchalance as her sons sat forward in their chairs. George muffled a small giggle. 'Oh, all right then.'

Lucy's tale:

'Did you see the little circles of mushrooms as we were walking into the forest?' asked Lucy.

'Dad said they were toadseats,' said Peter.

'That's almost right. They are called toadstools. Well remembered,' clarified George.

'Are they where toads come from?' asked Carl.

'Don't be stupid, toads come from the pond. Don't they dad?'

'Boys,' warned Lucy, 'No arguing. Now, are you going to listen to the story?' Both boys settled back into their chairs.

'Thank you. Now, you saw the toadstools and you saw how they formed circles? There was one circle of toadstools with a ring of large stone around it. Do you remember that one?' Both boys dutifully nodded at their mother as she continued, 'Well those are the doorways to the fairy realm. '

'Fairy realm?' Peter snorted.

'Let your mum tell her story,' George warned.

Lucy cleared her throat, pulling back their attention. 'Yes, they are doorways to the fairy realm. Now, fairies are about as long as your forearm, see that bit there,' Lucy gestured along her arm to show her sons how big fairies were before continuing, 'They have crazy hair and beautiful wings that let them fly where ever they want to go. The fairy realm is governed by a King and his name is King...' Lucy paused, a small smile on her lips as she looked at her sons with a raised eyebrow.

'King Peter,' yelled her eldest son.

'No, King Carl,' yelled her youngest.

Lucy allowed them to bicker for a moment more before her voice rose, drowning them out. 'The fairy realm was governed by King George.'

Her sons groaned and made retching noises. George smiled lovingly at his wife.

'Now, King George's father had two sons, Prince Orin and Prince Alston. Technically Prince Alston should have been king because he was the eldest, but King George saw the cruelty in Prince Alston, so even though he loved his son he realised it was better for his people if the crown went to his younger son Orin, who was a good, kind fairy.

'Prince Alston was very angry with his father for passing him over for his younger brother and plotted to kill them both. Going to the forest he collected poisonous berries and roots which he pressed into a paste. On the night when his father had arranged a big celebration meal to announce Prince Orin as his heir, Prince Alston took his chance. When his brother wasn't looking he prepared a special meal for King Orin and Prince Orin, slipping the paste into it, knowing that the minute it touched his father's and brother's lips, it would kill them immediately.

'King George sat at the head of the long table, his wife at his side while Prince Alston and the rest of the court took their seats. Prince Alston watched eagerly as King George raised his fork, not knowing that the food was tainted. However, just before it reached his lips, his dog jumped up, knocking the king's fork to the ground. King Orin began to tell off his dog, when he saw the poor animal spasm and die. Falling to the floor beside his beloved pet, the king lifted the dogs head and out fell the poisoned food. Prince Orin immediately knew it was his brother who tried to kill him and his father and drew his sword.

'Prince Alston, believing himself to be the better swordsman smiled at the challenge and drew his own sword. They ran at each other and none of the court could see who was winning, such was the blur from their swords. Their fight took them through the underground palace. Past the queen's bedroom, past the servants' quarters, through the throne room and around the treasure stacked in the safe. Just when Prince Alston thought he had won, Prince Orin would attack again with renewed energy and vice versa. On and on they fought for hours, for days.

'Eventually the brothers found their way to the doorway between realms and they fell through into the fairy circle in the human world where they continued their fight.

'Now, humans are not supposed to enter a fairy circle, it's said to be very bad luck but there were two very naughty boys,' Lucy looked at her sons, 'Called Peter and Carl who were in the forest that day.'

'We're not naughty boys mum,' squealed Carl while Peter shook his head.

'No you're not, but this Peter and Carl were very naughty boys indeed. They heard the swords clashing and wondered what was happening so imagine their surprise when they found the fairy circle and saw two fairies fighting in it! Prince Orin and Prince Alston were so intent on their fight that they didn't see the two naughty boys sneaking up on them until it was too late. Prince Orin was the first to react, sticking his sword into the hand of Peter, or was it Carl, so the boy pulled away, but Prince Alston was not so lucky. One of the boys grabbed Prince Alston as Prince Orin rushed through the doorway, sealing it with his magic so the boys could not follow.'

'And what happened to Prince Alston?' Carl asked breathlessly.

'What happens to all naughty, nasty people: he died a slow and painful death. The fairies never found him, but they did find bits of his wings for years afterwards, scattered all around the forest. Where the pieces of Prince Alston's wings landed, bluebells would grow. We can go and see the bluebells tomorrow and you can think about Prince Alston. It was said that the boys were part of a group of travellers who would pass this way every spring, bringing with them a little creature in a metal cage. A little creature who would weep about a realm he could never return to and a brother he had lost.'

'Ewww, that's gross mum,' laughed Carl.

'My turn,' called Peter, clearing his voice dramatically. Seeing Carl shiver, Lucy rose and pulled blankets from the tent. She handed one to George and tucked one around Carl who smiled sleepily. Peter carelessly threw the blanket around his shoulders, creating a cowl.

'OK Peter. What's your story about?' asked George. Surveying his family, George felt his heart bursting with love for them all. He was already planning what they would do tomorrow. There was an inflatable raft in the car which they might take out on the lake, then there were the fairy circles to investigate, bluebells to search for and he was certain the boys would want to look for the spring with water to make them invisible. He would have to remember to take his book of plants because he wanted to teach his sons which plants they could eat. It was going to be a busy day.

Peter's tale:

'I heard it off a boy at school,' Peter started excitedly.

'And what's it about?' asked Lucy, rubbing her hands to try and warm them.

'Werewolves!' said Peter, jumping from his chair. Carl barely registered his brother as sleep dragged his eyelids southwards. Lucy and George shared a wary glance.

'And what do these werewolves do?' Lucy asked cautiously.

'They kill people and tear out their guts and eat them,' explained Peter, hands flying for emphasis.

'I think that might be enough blood and gore for one

evening,' George climbed out of his chair and threw another log onto the fire. 'Time for bed.'

'But dad, I didn't get to tell my story,' whined Peter.

'I know Peter, but it's late and I promise you can tell us your story first thing tomorrow. When it's daylight and you won't get nightmares,' continued George firmly. He picked up the sleeping Carl and carried him towards the smaller tent.

'But mum,' Peter looked to his mother for assistance, but she shook her head firmly. 'Do as your dad says. It's bedtime now. You can tell your werewolf story in the morning. Go on, brush your teeth and then bed.'

'But Carl didn't brush his teeth.'

'Well I'm sure he'll brush them extra well in the morning. Go on Peter, I won't tell you again.'

Realising further argument was futile, Peter sulkily did as his mum ordered. With a little more fuss, Lucy and George managed to get their eldest son into his tent. After making sure both their sons were tucked into their sleeping bags, they zipped up the small tent and crossed the camp site to their own.

Lucy snuggled up close to her husband who wrapped his arms around her and sighed happily.

'It's been such a fun day, George, this was a fantastic idea. I think the boys are really enjoying being out in the wild and I know when they get back to school, knowing their imaginations, they will have seen that ghostly Robin Hood character of yours,' Lucy laughed softly and she felt George smile as he nuzzled into her hair.

'I'm just glad everyone's having fun. Camping's certainly changed since I did it with my father. We never had GPS to tell us if we were going off the trail, or air mattresses that inflated in 30 seconds, with gas fired BBQ's that clean themselves,' George continued to list the high-tech gadgets they had brought with them on the trip.

Lucy sighed dramatically but her voice showed her mirth, 'Oh here we go, in my day stories of hardship and back breaking work, hunting for your dinner and gutting it by hand. I've heard the stories George. I've also heard your dad's versions where your mum packed you both sandwiches and the only hunting you did was the time you lost your yo-yo.'

George moulded himself against his wife's back and snuggled into her hair. 'It was my favourite yo-yo,' he whispered as his fingers slowly travelled up Lucy's body.

'George, the boys,' whispered Lucy, her lips meeting her husband's as she turned to him.

'The boys won't hear a thing, I guarantee they are asleep dreaming of noble deeds and dripping ghosts,' George's kisses became more urgent.

Lucy suddenly pushed George away and sat up, fear lacing her voice, 'George, do you hear an animal outside?'

'Lucy, we're in the forest, we're surrounded by animals and they all come out at night. Come here.' Lucy slowly lay down beside her husband but a second later was sitting up again, flicking off the covers as she reached for a torch.

'There is was again. Didn't you hear it? It sounds like a dog or a wolf or something.'

George sighed, 'Now whose imagination is running wild? I'm going to have to go and look aren't I?' He started pulling on his jeans, flinging his bare feet into his walking boots. He took the torch from his wife, and reached for the zipper of the tent. Lucy watched him, her eyes fearful.

'Be careful,' she whispered.

George gave her a lopsided grin, 'Who's afraid of the big bad wolf?' he joked, pulling the tent closed behind him.

The Lake

The Lake is beautiful at this time of year. The leaves are just starting to turn, but there is enough green to make the pockets of rusty brown burst like fireworks. The sun warms my skin and I lie luxuriating in its glow. Autumn has always been my favourite season at the Lake. As I relax, taking in the tranquil surroundings, I turn to ask what her favourite time of year at the Lake is, but I'm guessing she doesn't feel the same about the Lake as I do. Looking at the expression on her face, I bite my lip and decide that some questions are better left unasked, so I return to looking at the lake, her tranquillity covering me like a blanket.

The hint of a breeze flutters the leaves and cools my skin. The Lake is wide, but from this position I can see all around. We're on the north bank, catching the dying sun as it glides across the sky in the south. Surprisingly, given its sunny position, this isn't a popular spot on the Lake because there are no inviting beaches and most of the ground is knotted with tree roots. The 'best' places are on the east and west of the Lake and those are always the most busy. There's even a cafe at one end and a restaurant on the opposite side which are always filled with people during the summer. However, it's all quiet now. The mass of people who jostle for space in the sticky summer sun have all returned to their lives in the city. Stuck in their office spaces, they can only dream of feeling the rejuvenating powers of the Lake. There are locals who know different hidden pockets around the Lake for weekend fishing, or an illicit late-night meeting. But for now, she is all ours and I selfishly guard her against intrusions.

There is a wooden swimming platform at the eastern end of the Lake. The platform has been there since before I was even born and the wood has been worn smooth by countless swimmers over the years. In peak season people swarm like bees for a space from which to watch the last honey rays of the summer sun. I'm tempted to suggest we swim out to watch the sunset but know she won't want to so, I don't break the silence between us. Thoughts and memories buzz like bees into my brain, of sunbathing on the platform next summer, and the summer after that. The Lake and all that is in her are constant.

Unchangeable.

The water has that crystal quality normally only reserved for Hollywood movies, and then only created on a computer. It constantly pulses back and forth like a heartbeat, caressing the neck of the shore. The water level is unusually high for this time of year. There were storms and a lot of rain recently which has boosted the water level, leaving the Lake swollen and full, pregnant and life giving. Close to the shore I can see tiny minnows bravely searching for food before fleeing as bigger fish glide closer to investigate the tiny electric pulses their prey give off with each beat of their hearts. Leaves have landed on her surface and drift aimlessly like boats willingly lost at sea. And who would not happily lose themselves on the Lake?

A splash!

I search for the source of the noise and see a fish jumping out of the water. I nudge her arm and gesture to the growing ripples as my eyes search for another jump. She ignores me as I point excitedly. The fish jumps again and the droplets of water fly high before becoming one with the Lake once more. Their presence can still be seen though as little ripples undulate out across the Lake, causing the fallen leaves to bob and dip uncertainly. The fish keeps jumping and from my position I can just make out a darker shape under the water, stalking it. One more splash and then silence.

All is not safe here at the Lake. Predators can appear and disappear, the Lake offering perfect camouflage within her embrace.

The recent rains have left a slightly damp mossy smell in the air but the ground is dry. I roll back onto my bed of leaves and stretch, easing the cramps in my arms and back. The recent exertion has tired me and I'm feeling knots in my muscles. I could ask her to rub them, but I know she'll say that I brought it on myself so not to complain. The sun filters through the leaves of the trees and permeates my bones, helping unwind the knots. I feel so relaxed, as if I could melt like ice cream and my body run down into the Lake.

With the sun behind them, the leaves become x-rays and I can see their veins sending life-giving nutrients right to the tips. The breeze has dropped but the leaves are moving of their own accord. I wonder why they do that? Even on clear and motionless days leaves move on their own. It's almost as if they are jealous of those animals that can move freely, without being held to the ground by roots. Perhaps they feel that if even one leaf can move, the rest of the tree will follow. The leaves at the Lake which have turned their various shades of red and brown cling stubbornly to the branches. They spin and shiver as if they know death is only a short time away and they need to enjoy the tiny amount of life they have left. The breeze rises again and forces one leaf to give up its struggle. It pops off the branch, circling slowly down to the expectant, welcoming surface of the Lake.

I sit up as I catch movement out of the corner of my eye. It's a line of ants, marching to their own rhythm. I skip along the ranks to discover their destination. Frowning, I see they are making their way towards a discarded cola can. It rises like a red pimple on the otherwise perfect complexion of the Lakeside.

She ignores me as I crawl after them, but I can almost feel the contemptuous roll of her eyes. I watch as each ant collects a ball of sugary liquid in its pincer jaws before setting off again on its return journey to the nest. Taking the base of the can I upend it, shaking out the last residue of the dark drink. The sickly smell of the drink mixes with the smell of decay as mouldy leaves drop from the can. Some ants fall from the can as well, landing awkwardly amongst their brothers. There is chaos in the squad of ants as they run in all directions. However, as with all disciplined creatures, order is quickly restored and they soon fall back into line, with scouts leading them on to their next mission. I return to my spot in the sun and carefully place the empty can in my bag, ready to recycle. Nothing should detract from the pure beauty of the Lake.

High above, floating in and out of the spotlight of the sun is a bird of prey, its long black wings barely moving as it catches the wind. Its head scans back and forth as it looks for prey. It stares at me for a while, sizing up if I am within its range. I stare back unblinking. The sun burns my eyes as the bird moves out of its way. Seeing something which obviously takes its fancy, a slight change in the arch of its tail and it's gliding in ever smaller circles. For a second it seems to hang motionless in the air, suspended by magic before the stronger force of gravity takes over and it plunges towards the Lake. Head down, wings tucked close to its body it's the perfect hunting machine. I sit up in time to see it grab a large fish from the Lake. The Lake doesn't even have enough time to form a reflection of the bird before it's spreading its wings and effortlessly taking flight once more to the shelter of the trees. I wonder if the large fish dripping from its claws is the one I saw hunting the minnows.

Hunter and hunted. How those roles merge here at the lake.

There is movement in the trees behind me. I turn languidly. I cock my ear like a dog, trying to pinpoint where the noise came from. Nothing. My mind skips from one topic to the next while she is wrapped in her own silent thoughts. There is another loud crack. I immediately focus on the source of the noise as it bounces around the Lake. The echo would prove disorientating for most people, but I am used to the noises of the forest and like the bird of prey searching for its next victim, I scan the area where the noise came from.

I am absolutely still.

I know we are exposed here on the shore, but the best view of the Lake is from here and in my excitement I had forgotten some of my usual caution. She doesn't react. I'm not sure she heard anything, but then she doesn't have my skill. I force myself to breathe through my nose to stop the sound of my ragged breath. The pounding in my chest is sending blood rushing to my ears, making it difficult to hear anything.

Wait!

There it is again. There is definitely something watching me. I feel like my heart will burst through my chest, it is pounding so hard. One part of my mind is racing about possible threats and the other is making plans of escape, discarding them as quickly as it is thinking of them. I carefully shuffle my feet under me, ready to leap up as I continue studying every detail of the tree line. Just then a young deer breaks his cover and comes to the Lake side for a drink. He regards me with curiosity, completely unthreatened. Tiny horns are pushing through like buds in spring. I relax and my breathing returns to normal as I slouch back. The sun bounces from the water and blinds me momentarily. I pat her arm reassuringly but her senses aren't as keen as mine and I'm sure she didn't even hear the deer.

Rolling onto my side, I look at her and smile lovingly. I am still a little blinded from the bright sun. Sunlight pushes its way through the skeleton leaves, catching the highlights in her hair. I look at her through half-closed eyes. The sunlight from her hair forms a halo. She's an angel now, not always, but the Lake has transformed her. I look down into her eyes as a bubble forms on her lips and bursts. I cannot believe how much love I feel for her, lying beside me.

Sharing this special time at the Lake together.

There is a mosquito buzzing around her head but she makes no move to swat it away. It lands on her cheek and its body slowly swells as it sucks her blood. She doesn't flinch as I grab the insect between my thumb and forefinger and pluck it from her cheek. A small drop of blood oozes out and, licking my thumb, I wipe it away. The pinkness of the blood merges with the flush of her cheeks.

I caress her face with the back of my hand, slowly trailing it down her soft neck. I make little circles as I continue down, catching my finger slightly as it nudges her shirt, green with tiny pink flowers, exposing forbidden flashes of skin. Blue veins stand out against her pale skin like the x-rayed leaves of the trees which protect our liaison from unwelcome intrusion. She doesn't move but her breathing becomes more shallow. I give her a shy smile as my fingers walk their way over the buttons of her blouse. She sucks in her breath in anticipation but continues to lie motionless as my fingers pluck teasingly at the flimsy fabric of her blouse, moving south.

My fingers stop their teasing.

I slowly grip the bone handled knife embedded in her chest as a gurgling escapes her dry lips. The contours of the handle perfectly fit my fingers after years of use. Pulling, the knife sticks. It's caught on bone. Twisting it anti-clockwise I hear the bone grating, but the knife comes loose. Congealed blood claws at the knife, not wanting to let it go, but eventually cracks as I slowly pull. Blood emerges from her chest and spills over, joining the small red lake around her body. The smell of metallic death fills my nostrils. The shirt is glued to the knife and rises along with the blade.

One final tug and the blade is free of the shirt. Some of the pale green fibres have stuck to the blade, the blood makes it look rusty. Shaking my head at this unacceptable mess, I wander down to the Lakeside. The mud sucks at my boots as I squat and wash my knife. Look after your knife and it will look after you is a proverb I live by. I tear some grass to dry it as I walk back to her. Dropping down I watch as her hand spasms up and down, shivering like the leaves on the trees. Is she trying to tell me something? Some hidden secret? I don't know and she's certainly not in the mood to explain.

Studying her face I focus on her eyes. Her eyes tell me so much. About her family who will now be missing her. About friends she will never see again. Of passionate arguments and petty romance. It's clichéd to say that the eyes are the window to the soul but they are the windows through which we see the world and I wonder what she is looking at right now as she looks past me. I follow her eyes. She is staring straight up, as I was earlier, looking through the leaves at the life-giving, energising sun above. With a final childlike gurgling noise her chest stops moving and dullness drifts from her eyes, enveloping her body.

A single tear has fallen down her cheek. It reminds me of the small rivers which feed the Lake as it mingles with the blood in her hair.

Lifting her ankles, I walk back to the Lake shore. She flops about behind me over the rough roots like a fish out of water. The mud clings to my boots, pulling me in, not wanting me to leave, daring me to defy the wants and needs of the Lake. I fight against the clawing mud and the tide which tries to trip me as I plunge into my mistress. The Lake can be mischievous in her attentions.

I brush her hair back from her face as she slides into the Lake. The water quickly covers her in a special embrace as she bobs on the surface like autumn leaves before silver fingers encircle her body, slowly dragging her under the surface. With a final look, I leave the soothing clutches of the Lake.

Once more I lie back on my bed of leaves and enjoy my solitude and the view of the Lake.

All is quiet.
All is still.
Here at the Lake.

The Dragon Tree

Hopes and seeds were sown,
Couples danced and sang,
Their future unknown,
Their dreams their only plan
The day the dragon fell to earth.

All the town was there,
Enjoying the summer sun,
The villagers were at the fair,
Except the farmer's son,
The day the dragon fell to earth.

In the forest was dark, foreboding,
Its depths silent, un-tread,
Trees gnarled and
His jumper bobbing red,
The day the dragon fell to earth.

Boy, the farmer's son,
The bullies tortured for fun
Boy hid within the woods,
But there was nowhere to run,
The day the dragon fell to earth.

The sun formed a spotlight,
In the clearing of the trees,
The bullies surrounded Boy,
He looked at them, all three,
The day the dragon fell to earth.

Suddenly from up on high,
A darkness came,
And blocked the sky,
The bullies stopped their game,
The day the dragon fell to earth.

A mighty crash, bang, boom,
Bullies and Boy looked at rising dust,

And emerged from the gloom,
A dragon coloured rust,
The day the dragon hit the earth.

The bullies scattered, running scared,
Leaving Boy alone
They didn't care how he fared,
Alone in the forest, filled with insect drone,
The day the dragon fell to earth.

The dragon stood tall,
His wings flashed wide,
With his first steps, fall!
He landed at Boy's side,
The day the dragon fell to earth.

The dragon's mouth opened wide,
Boy saw the fire burning deep,
As the dragon sighed,
Out his nostrils the fire did seep.
The day the dragon fell to earth.

Boy held out his hand,
The dragon's face to touch,
His skin coarse sand,
Under Boys hand was rough,
The day the dragon fell to earth.

The dragon snorted warmly
Sparks shooting from his nose,
Scorching Boy's skin,
Singeing all his clothes,
The day the dragon fell to earth.

Boy kept the dragon safe,
As storm clouds pulled summer away,
The changing of the seasons,
Seemed to happen in the course of a day,
The day the dragon fell to earth.

The years passed by,
And the dragon grew large and strong,

Bond between dragon and boy
As strong as Boy's white beard was long
The day the dragon fell to earth.

One day Boy didn't visit,
As he always had,
The dragon sniffed the air,
Searching for his friend,
The day the dragon fell to earth.

Boy never returned,
The dragon left lost and alone,
He didn't understand,
His whimper turned to moan
The day the dragon fell to earth.

The rain flowed down,
And touched the dragon's skin,
The dragon opened his mouth,
And the water flowed in,
The day the dragon fell to earth.

The water drowned the dragon,
Taking away his flame,
Darkness filled the dragon,
But soon he felt no pain,
The day the dragon died on earth.

The water hammered down,
And slowly the dragon did harden,
From scaly tail tip to glowing snout,
The fire slowly burned out,
The day the dragon died.

And now in the forests there,
Stands a dragon tree,
Its branches tall and wide,
Frozen in time forever more,
The day the dragon died.

The Bridge

'That all you brought? 'nother scrawny lamb?' sneered Zulrisi to her husband, Trolgar, who stood forlorn by the side of the bridge, the bedraggled lamb hanging limply from his long bare arm and dragging slightly in the muddy trickle that passed for a river.

'But people was der. They see me,' he muttered. 'They set their dog on me. See?'

Trolgar turned around so that Zulrisi could see the large dog bite on her husband's bottom.

'You is troll. You eat da dog, you kill da human. You doan run way with little lamb,' Zulrisi threw her hands in the air in exasperation.

'I doan like new humans. Old humans fun. Could play games on them, chase them out of forest, eat der babies but new humans, they not frightened of trolls no more,' Trolgar slumped down, causing a splat in the mud as he hit the squishy surface. His head was large, almost too large for his body, with moss and twigs sticking out of his long tangle of grey hair which trailed down his back. The green-grey skin under his brown eyes sagged almost to the bottom of his bulbous nose and two large canine teeth stuck up from his bottom jaw. Coils of skin drooped under his chin onto his rotund belly and his short legs were covered in wiry hair. His skinny arms reached his knees and were topped by short black claws.

'They no frightened cos you not frightening no more. I think you getting old, Trolgar,' groused Zulrisi. She was almost the spitting image of her husband, but two sagging breasts flopped over her belly, her hair was a shade lighter than her husband's and her knees were less hairy. 'If I see da humans, I'll chase 'em. I growl at 'em. I no run away. Stupid Trolgar and now all we eat is lamb. I 'member when we eat the humans. Put them in the pot wiv garlic or if you pulled off the head and squeezed out their insides.' Zulrisi drooled at the memory. Turning to her husband, her eyes narrowed. 'You go again, go get me human for dinner.'

Trolgar shook his head. 'Is no good I tells you. Da new humans is harder to kills. 'Member 'ow it used to be? When they all lived in da mud wiv us?'

Zulrisi nodded sagely. 'Was good den. We eats lots of humans. They never fights back and all they have is little stabby swords. Those not hurt Trolgar. Now, they no frightened.' Zulrisi trailed off. She looked at her husband, 'But Trolgar get fat. Lazy too. Trolgar needs to be strong troll and kill da humans so Zulrisi can cook them.

Trolgar looked at his wife. 'Maybe Zulrisi comes wiv Trolgar. We frightens good together.'

'No Trolgar!' Zulrisi snapped. 'We agreed: you hunt, I cook. You know what happened last time. So you go hunt.' Zulrisi tried to wave Trolgar out from under the bridge and into the growing drizzle.

'Bet I be better at cooking than Zulrisi,' groused Trolgar. He started to shuffle away, his claws dragging in the mud. Rivulets of water bubbled to the surface and flowed after him.

'You say Zulrisi no good at cooking?' howled Zulrisi, waving an old sheep bone at her husband. He ignored her: it was an argument they had had many times. 'I no like lamb, I like human. I no make lamb taste good. Lamb always taste like dirt.'

'Cos you cook wiv dirt,' mumbled Trolgar as his wife glared at him.

Zulrisi followed her husband to the edge of the bridge, dropping the bone into the rapidly bogging mud. She looked at her husband with momentary tenderness. Pulling a decaying pigeon from his tangle of beard she popped it in her mouth, chewing thoughtfully.

'Trolgar no go alone. We goes together and we eat da people,' she suggested, her claws encircling his as he gazed down at her, snot dripping from the end of his nose.

'Da new humans is strong Zulrisi, and no frightened of trolls. We must be clever,' said Trolgar. Zulrisi let out a long fart while her husband picked twigs from his hair, then both trolls looked out into the rain through a green haze. Trolgar sniffed and grunted before farting himself, longer and louder than his wife.

'Together we can kill them. I gots wild garlic and da roots of da weeping willow from da lake. Those is very good because the sacrifice cried all over dem, so is extra juicy,' mulled Zulrisi, her mouth drooling and the drool making its way down her plump belly.

Trolgar sighed, 'Is dat time of year again? Da time for sacrifice? Always such shame. Da young life, stopped so sudden. All the blood. And all go to stupid lake gods. No one sacrifice to us. Would save time of hunting,' he grumbled.

'How many years we seen da sacrifice?' Zulrisi asked. She smiled up at her husband. 'Always we live here, under bridge. Together.'

Trolgar gave her hand a squeeze, their claws scratching against each other. 'Been here long time. Now, I gets hungry. Zulrisi come with me and we go eat humans? I see some camping near stone circle.'

'No! We no go near fairies. Not after what they do to Zulrisi last time,' Zulrisi looked at a patch of bald skin on her wobbling belly where the hair had never grown back. She shuddered at the memory.

'We go other camp site. I smelled juicy humans der. And I hears more childrens coming up the track. I bets they go up the mountain. We could kills them all and wouldn't need to hunt again in long time.' Both Trolgar and Zulrisi's eyes gleamed with greed and their bellies grumbled.

Zulrisi flexed her chipped claws and picked a little grass from between her teeth. 'I excited to go hunting. Know is Trolgar's job but used to enjoy. Zulrisi no go since fairies but today Zulrisi gets claws bloody and tastes real human flesh again.'

Trolgar smiled at his wife, brown stubs of teeth just showing in the damp grey light. Suddenly he grabbed at her hand but she had moved so he ended up knocking her drooping breast, sending it squelching into her belly. She looked at him, startled by his sudden movements.

'What problem, Trolgar?' she asked.

'You hear?' he whispered. Zulrisi moved closer to her husband so the hair on their bellies tangled.

'What?' she replied.

Trolgar shushed her with a wave of his claw and listened again for a moment. He looked at her excitedly. 'I thinks they come to us. I thinks the humans is walking this way. We set trap and we kills them all. Youse stand on da other side of bridge and jumps out. Then we grabs em and kills em. Humans gonna be so much better than lamb.'

Zulrisi nodded and stepped over the shallow river to the other side of the bridge so she was only a few metres apart from Trolgar. She nodded at him as they both listened to the approaching humans.

'Keep up boys,' said an authoritative female voice, 'I know it's damp but we're nearly at the camp site. Just a short hike up the mountain and we're there. Now, be careful crossing the bridge, it's likely to be slippery in this weather. Over a thousand years old and lots of different stories associated with it.'

One of the boys following the scout leader snorted, 'But Miss, you said that about the old tree and that ring of stones. All silly old stories.'

'Don't say that, Tony,' replied the scout leader. 'These woods are filled with history and I'm certain we're going to see lots of evidence of it during this camping trip. Now, line up and let's get across this bridge. Angus, your sleeping bag is coming loose. Tighten those straps or it will...' she didn't need to finish her sentence as the boy's sleeping bag fell from his rucksack and slid down towards the river and under the bridge.

Trolgar gestured for his wife to get ready, flexing his claws and slamming his jaws together in expectation. Zulrisi grinned at him as she practiced swiping and stretched her muscles, ready to attack. She nodded to show she was ready as the little red covered sleeping bag came to a stop near Trolgar's feet.

He grinned as a small boy skidded down the river bank

and the sounds of 'Go and collect that Angus,' were dying out.

Trolgar shook his head so his hair was especially spiky and bared his teeth while he struck a pose with both sets of claws raised threateningly. It was his most scary pose and one he knew would scare little Angus, wiping the mud from his hands onto his trousers.

Angus looked up and saw the troll. He slipped backwards for a moment and opened his mouth to scream. Trolgar's smile broadened and he flicked his claws to scare the boy. He saw Zulrisi raise her claws out of the corner of his eye.

Angus paused, his mouth opening and closing like a fish as Trolgar readied to strike. Angus moved for his pocket and Trolgar paused as he expected a weapon to be drawn: he wanted to fully take stock of his victim before he attacked.

However, it wasn't a knife that Angus pulled from his damp trouser pocket but his mobile phone. Lifting it in front of him there was a bright flash and Trolgar fell backwards, into the mud. Zulrisi rushed to her husband's side.

'Hey guys,' shouted Angus to his fellow scouts on the bridge. 'Come look at this. There's some funny creatures down here.' Angus continued clicking photos on his mobile phone. Soon the rest of the scout troop had slid down the river bank and were taking photos of the two trolls while their scout master tried to get them into some order and on with their journey.

Zulrisi hugged her husband, 'Trolgar, what's happening?'

'I no know,' groaned Trolgar as another flash blinded him. He cowered down into the mud, wrapping himself around Zulrisi, and occasionally swiping at the boys with his claws, but without much enthusiasm.

Finally the boys stopped taking their photos and, still giggling, they left Trolgar and Zulrisi alone under the bridge.

Trolgar prised himself from Zulrisi's vice like grip. She looked up at him, the terror still in her muddy eyes. 'What was that?' she asked.

Trolgar peeked out from under the bridge to confirm the noisy boys had left. 'New humans. I tol' you they no frightened trolls no more. Now they have bright, loud weapons. Trolgar no like.'

Zulrisi smiled at her husband as she picked up the lamb he had brought in earlier. 'I cooks lamb for dinner. Trolgar brings me good lamb I like. Lamb tastes good.'

Trolgar grinned his brown smile at his wife. 'And Zulrisi cooks good lamb,' he replied.

The Mountain

Transcript of conversation between the Rescue Base and Chopper One. The Rescue Base had received a report that a troop of scouts had become lost due to rapidly deteriorating conditions. The plan had been for them to hike through the forest, then camp on the mountain, earning different merit badges, before returning home the following day. However, nothing had been heard of them and five hours after they were due to return home, the Mountain Rescue Team received a call. They scrambled a helicopter and headed out to the mountain to try and find the troop.

'Base, this is chopper one.'

'Chopper one this is Base. Please state your location.'

'Base we are approximately five minutes away from destination. Over.'

'Chopper one. Confirm when arrived. Over.'

Interference

'Repeat Chopper One. What's your visual?'

'Base. There's a fog. It's coming out of the trees. I've not seen fog like this before. Wait. There's something there. I can see shapes in the fog. Base, do you copy?'

'Copy Chopper One. Are you clear to set down?'

'Yes. We can set down a little further up the mountain. The fog seems to have stopped at tree line. Must be some atmospheric thing. It's always crazy up here. Remember last week, that sudden snow storm? Middle of summer and the snow hits. Ok Base, we've located a spot to set down. Sending you our coordinates now. Base, we are clear to set down.'

'Received Chopper One. We have your location.'

'Base, we have set down. Will maintain radio contact while we assess the area. Moving into the forest now.'

'Understood Chopper One. Over.'

'Base. We have found evidence of a camp. I repeat. We have located their camp. We are assessing the equipment. Over.'

'Copy. What have you found Chopper One? From the

reports we received it was a group of six children, repeat six children, aged between seven and ten. Also, two adults, one male and one female were leading the group. Repeat, one male, one female.'

'Base, there is evidence someone was here. There's the start of a camp fire— firewood and tinder but no evidence it was lit. The cooler box is un-opened but someone was drinking a soft drink— the top is off and it's spilled over the floor. There's also seven tents: six singles and one two man. I think this is our group Base, as there are Scout badges sewn on the cover of a backpack in one of the tents. However, none of the tents have been fully erected. There's also footprints on the canvas as if they were running over them. Some sort of game perhaps while they were setting up?'

'Never played those sorts of games when I was a scout, Chopper One. Rules were we set up camp quickly, then the fun started. Have you found anything else? Can you confirm this is the camp we are looking for?'

'Understood Base. We have found six backpacks further down the slope. I think this is our group— the badges identify them as troop one-eight-one.'

'Chopper One. Any sign of the group?'

'Negative Base. All the equipment looks abandoned. I don't know what happened up here but they left a mess. Henson's just found a woggle. Base, this is our troop's camp but not a clue where they have gone. Could they have taken a walk?

'I don't believe they would have left their camp as you've described it, Chopper One. To have left all their equipment? Sounds like they left in a hurry. Can you see any explanation about why they might have left?'

Pause

'Base. Please repeat. We're getting some interference up here. I think it's the fog. We're getting deep in the trees. What's that? Base we have found what looks to be a child's watch. There's blood on the face and the hands have stopped at fourteen-hundred hours. Repeat fourteen-hundred. That's about the time they were due to leave, isn't it?'

'That's right Chopper One. Their ETD was two pm, to arrive in the car park for collection by parents at four. What else do you see?'

'Base, I think we're going to have to return when the conditions are better: bring the dogs up here. We can't see much. Light is fading and the fog is getting worse.'

'OK, Chopper One. I'll notify the dog team. It might be that they can hike in to the spot and start the search tonight. With the temperature dropping, I'm not sure those kids will survive the night if they're not properly kitted out. Spookiest weather I've ever experienced in summer.'

'That's a negative, Base. The fog is so thick up here, they wouldn't see anything and the dogs would get lost. In fact, Henson! Hey, Henson, where are you? Henson, that you? Base, I've lost Henson. I think I can see him among the trees.'

Transmission lost

'Chopper One. Chopper One, come in please. Chopper One. Do you read?'

Silence

'Base. Base, do you read? Henson has found one of the boys. He's suffering hypothermia, dehydration and blood loss. We are returning to the chopper now.'

'Fantastic news Chopper One. Does the boy have any idea where the rest of the group are?'

'Base?
Transmission lost

'Chopper One. Please repeat. We are experiencing a lot of static and cannot hear you.'

Silence

'Chopper One. Switch to channel five. We are experiencing severe interference.'

Feedback

'Base, do you copy? Over? Base we can see a lot of blood but no bodies. Please confirm that we are here to collect survivors.'

'We copy, Chopper One. Good to hear your voice. Have you returned to the chopper?'

'Base, we are having trouble locating the chopper. We are

continuing to walk uphill but I think we walked further into the forest than we realised. The fog's coming in pretty think. It's hard to see anything.'

'Understood Chopper One. What about the boy? What's his condition? Has he said anything?'

'Base, we are having trouble hearing you. I hope you *transmission lost**. The boy *transmission lost** name is *transmission lost**. Base, do you read? He says they came *transmission lost**. Claims they *static**. It's the trees Base. They're in the trees.'

'Chopper One. Chopper One. Come in please. What is in the trees? Repeat, what is in the trees?'

Silence

'Oh god. Base? They're here. They took Henson. Repeat, Henson is down. I've got the boy and am running back to the chopper but I can hear them behind me. I can't—' **transmission lost**

'Chopper One. Please come in. What the hell is going on up there? And what's this about things in the trees? Where's Henson? Do you think this is some sort of game? Come in. Repeat, Chopper One. Come in.'

'Base, there's something here. Something I can't see, but it's in the trees. I got separated from the boy. He was shouting for a minute but I can't hear him *transmission lost**'

'Chopper One. Have you got back to the chopper? Can you take off? Return to Base. I repeat, get your arse out of there ASAP.'

'**Static** -it. Base. Gah! Base. They are in the trees. Don't *transmission lost**. Base, tell Lorna I love her.'

'Chopper One? Chopper One. Come in. Chopper One. What do we do? Chopper One?'

Silence
Silence

The Stone Circle

'It's hardly been studied since it was found,' Jen enthused as Landon followed behind, carrying a large case of equipment. 'Stone circles have been found all over the UK and Ireland. They are part of its culture, its heritage. The Rollright Stones in Oxfordshire, Doll Tor in Derbyshire, Callanish stone circle in the Outer Hebrides, Druid's Circle in Wales, the Stallmoor and Merivale stone rows in Dartmoor and those are just some of the lesser known ones. Let's not forget about the important sites at Stonehenge and Avebury. This is our chance to be there at the beginning, before anyone else has trampled all over the site and ruined the evidence.'

'What makes you think no-one else had already vandalised this site?' asked Landon wearily as he dropped the box on the ground and collapsed on top of it.

Jen scowled at him, but Landon was too tired to even look sheepish and droplets of doubt started to drip on her confidence. Then she turned back to the ring of stones and her enthusiasm returned.

'It's been suggested that Crick Stone in Cornwall has curative powers and it's supposed to get its name from its ability to cure the crick in a back or other part of the body. Most of the stones here are flat and smooth but I wonder if they were a primitive form of massage. There could once have been ground so that bits of the stone protruded, perhaps to fit with a person's pressure points. The sick or injured could then lie on the stones as a kind of reflexology,' said Jen.

'Now you're sounding like a new age hippy. If I find a tie-dyed t-shirt in this box, I'm going home,' groused Landon.

'It's a legitimate theory. You should have read some of the ideas that have been suggested for Stonehenge's origins. And don't even get me started about aliens,' Jen said, only partly joking.

Landon chuckled to himself as he started unpacking the equipment, laying it on the ground with precision.

Jen continued in a defensive tone, 'Just because people

didn't live in heated flats with plasma TV's playing their Wii's doesn't mean they were stupid. If nothing else they were closer to the earth, more understanding of the seasons and working with nature than we are with all our technology.'

'Sounds like you admire them,' Landon started in a cautious tone; he knew from experience how one of these types of conversations with Jen could go and after carrying the heavy box into the forest, he didn't have the patience or the energy to deal with it.

'Don't be ridiculous,' snapped Jen as she began snapping the pieces of equipment together. Well, just think, medical science has been doing research into ancient Chinese medicine and found positive benefits so there's something to be learned from the past. Now, I know you don't believe in ley lines,' started Jen.

'Hey! You don't believe in ley lines either. Don't start spouting mumbo-jumbo. You know that you just have to draw a line anywhere on a map of the UK and you'll hit any number of ancient sites, creating a so-called ley line,' interrupted Landon.

Jen sighed, 'I know. I know. But what I was going to say was, those ancient peoples knew something. Did you know that the level of knowledge of doctors in the roman period was not matched again until the beginning of the twentieth century. Are you really telling me that we have reached the pinnacle of our knowledge? Because I bet the Romans did. And they ended up forgetting it all.'

'And you want to remind them?' asked Landon.

Jen grinned at him. 'Yep, that's about it. Now, what do you think we should start with?' Jen reached into her backpack and pulled out maps, notes and articles, spreading them across the ground. 'It's really strange, but I tried to pull some of the pictures of this area off of the internet, you know Google maps and stuff but seems like the satellites can't get a decent image for some reason. It's so strange, I must have checked about half a dozen websites and no luck.'

Landon gave her a wry grin, 'Are you trying to tell me this

is England's answer to the Bermuda triangle? Are we about to experience ghost ships and stuff?'

Jen didn't look up from her maps, 'Don't be stupid. Now look, I've...'

'Well if the area is as kooky as you say, I don't think the magnetometer will be much use,' Landon said thoughtfully, his eyes roaming over the area.

'Really? But we carried it all this way,' groaned Jen.

Landon shrugged, 'There's an easy way to check. Pass me that box, it's got a compass in it.' Landon retrieved the small compass from the box and studied it for a moment before showing it to Jen. 'See? It's just spinning around. Too much background interference: we won't get any decent readings.'

'Damn,' muttered Jen.

Landon thought for a moment. 'Look, the daylight is starting to go a little. Perhaps we should set up the tents. We can check out your maps and stuff over dinner, then decide on the best way to assess the site. We can start early.'

'Blimey, you're right. See I told you strange things happened around here. It shouldn't get dark for another two hours or so,' exclaimed Jen.

Landon looked up into the trees at the rapidly declining sunlight. 'I'm not sure if it's the sun going down or if it's just the fog. Look at that! It's really...' Landon searched for a word.

'Strange?' offered Jen.

Landon rolled his eyes. 'Ok, ok, you got me. There is something strange about this place. You happy? Now, if we can get the camp sorted out, we can start working out how strange this place is.'

They worked hastily to set up the camp: the drop in temperature keeping them motivated to work quickly. Once the tents were up and they had a small fire blazing to burn off the damp night air, they settled down and reviewed the maps.

'See, the stone circle is here, in the clearing. It's surrounded by trees, and there's no evidence of settlements nearby, even further up the mountain where the trees thin out. What's really surprising because there are so many natural resources close by: the lake is here, access to the old roadways is here, there's the swamp area of course but they could possibly have drained that for farmland. There's no reason for them not to have built a settlement here,' Jen said.

'Yeah, I know but there could have been any number of reasons why they chose not to live here. Population was relatively sparse, so they would obviously choose to settle in areas closer to natural resources and more easy to defend.' Landon straightened out one of the maps, leaning closer to study the features more closely.

'OK, so they didn't want to live here, but why then build the stone circle? None of the stones are local rock. In fact, I got a friend at the university to test a sample of the rock I collected on my first trip. She said it was carried here, over two hundred miles. Can you believe it? The same thing happened at other stone circles. So what's the significance of these sites? Why would they put so much effort into creating sites, sourcing and dragging stones hundreds of miles, if they didn't hold some great significance?'

'And you think it's something to do with healing?' Landon was sceptical. His thesis at university had been the debunking of ancient myths. His disbelief had been one of the reasons why Jen has asked him on the trip: if she could convince Landon of her discovery then the rest of the scientific world would be easy.

Jen smiled, 'What's the saying? "There's stranger things in heaven and hell, Horatio, than you can dream of."'

'Not quite Shakespeare but ok, point taken.' Landon turned back to the maps of the area, 'I'd recommend we fully map the site tomorrow. Hopefully if we get an early start we can begin to clear some of the larger weeds off the stones by lunchtime and perhaps get a clearer idea of what we're dealing with. It looks like a fairly big site. How on earth did you find it? It's not exactly on the tourist route through the forest.'

Colour flushed Jen's cheeks. 'You wouldn't believe me if I told you,' she said quietly, looking into the flames.

'Hey, as long as it wasn't something kooky like you dreamt of the site then that's ok.' Landon's head snapped up when

Jen didn't answer. 'Shit. You're joking me. I'm here because of a dream? I cannot believe you dragged me up here, into the middle of fucking nowhere because of a dream. Do you seriously expect the academic community to believe anything you say if this gets out?' Landon paused in his ranting while Jen barely suppressed a smirk. 'What?' he demanded.

Jen burst out laughing. 'I never dreamed about the site. However, seeing your face, I kind of wished I had. No, I'd heard rumours in town that there was an old stone circle up here. There's lots of folk-tales about it: stories of battling brothers, fairies and stuff. All lots of nonsense of course but enough to get the locals wound up. I don't think anyone's been up here for years and when I asked about it, they actually warned me away from the place! Told me there was an old evil up here. Who knows, but hopefully if we make some real discoveries we can at least show the locals that their old beliefs are crazy.'

'You're all heart, doing all this work for the community,' sulked Landon. 'So the locals knew about this place but were too scared to visit? That makes no sense. It's beautiful up here and surely the local school would be interested in coming up and exploring their past. Thought you Brits were all about the history.'

'While you Yanks are desperate to actually have one,' quipped Jen. 'I don't know. The whole area is filled with such a mix of different stories and superstitions, from ghosts supposedly haunting the stones, to missing children taken by the trees. It's all nonsense.'

'So are you here to prove or disprove all those stories?' asked Landon.

Jen frowned. 'What do you mean? I'm a scientist. I'm here to disprove the crazy stuff and prove the sensible.'

'So healing stones is sensible but creatures in the forest are crazy? I'll never understand you Brits and your sense of humour.'

Jen grinned as she watched the flames dancing in the fire.

There was a crawling mist the next day as Landon and

Jen emerged from their tents. Hugging themselves to try and drive out the cold, Jen hastily rebuilt the fire until it was blazing.

'Hey, did you get up in the night? I thought I heard someone outside my tent,' asked Jen.

Landon shook his head. 'No, I was, what's the phrase, cream crackered? By the time I crawled into my sleeping bag I passed straight out,' replied Landon.

Jen frowned. 'I'm sure I heard something,' she muttered.

'Perhaps it was all a dream,' teased Landon. Either that or those fairy folk were out and about, just like the stories say.'

Jen stuck her tongue out at him.

The day quickly disappeared as Landon and Jen measured the distance between the stones, clearing some moss to see if there were markings underneath and then mapping them. They tried to use their equipment but nothing seemed to work when it was brought close to the stones.

'Cheap-ass university shitty equipment,' growled Landon, kicking at the equipment with his shoe.

Jen squatted next to the ground penetrating radar, fiddling with the controls. 'I don't understand. I checked it all before we left. It should be working.'

Landon sighed in frustration. 'Let's be honest Jen, it's not just the GPR. It's the photography equipment, the magnetometer, everything that runs on electricity is not working.'

Jen gave him a small smile, 'Well at least I went old school and brought my other camera. Hopefully I got some good shots but we will see when I develop the film.'

'I didn't understand why you bought that film camera with you but I'm glad you did or the whole trip would have been a waste.'

'I get a better contrast than with the digital. Look, let's get this stuff back to camp. At least we can look at the map we've created of the stones, as well as some of the etchings I managed to get off of them. I think it might be a basic language, perhaps like the Ogham.'

'I didn't think the Irish made it over here? And certainly if the site is as old as you're postulating, then it can't be the

Ogham since it was created around the fourth century,' said Landon.

'Blimey, Landon, we might have found something older than the Ogham. Can you imagine it? We'll be famous!'

'Don't get too excited just yet. It's not confirmed. We've still got a lot of work to do.'

'Just think, if it is, we might get a whole wing of the new archaeology building named after us. There'll be papers to write, conferences to attend,' Jen's eyes sparkled as she thought of the possibilities their discovery might offer them.

'Listen Jen, this morning you thought we were looking for magic, medicinal stones, now you're convinced they're an ancient form of language no one's discovered before. You know we can't make assertions in the field. We need to be cautious,' warned Landon.

Jen waved him off as they entered their camp. She was about to say something when she slowly looked around.

'What the....' she started.

'What's up?' asked Landon as he carefully stacked the equipment behind Jen. He took in the scene, 'Hey, what the hell? Who's been here?' he demanded.

The camp had been torn apart. Pieces of equipment lay on the ground, while all their belongings were strewn around. Their tents were still standing but they could see some large slashes in them. Jen quickly checked their tents while Landon snatched their belongings from out of trees and picked up clothes that had been thrown on the floor.

'Well nothing seems to have been taken,' said Jen as she slowly stood up when something on the tree behind her tent caught her eye. 'What the hell is this?' she asked, stepping over the ropes of her tent. Frowning she reached up to touch the letters scratched into the bark.

LEAVE

'Something really weird is going on. I think we should get out of here,' muttered Landon.

'Are you kidding me? Landon, we might be on for the discovery of the decade and you're worried about a few kids messing with our stuff and trashing the site?'

'It's not just kids messing, Jen. It's having our camp torn to shreds, it's having threatening messages carved into trees, it's having creatures sniffing outside our tents at night.'

Jen's head snapped up and she looked at Landon. 'You said you didn't hear anything last night,' she said.

Landon threw his notebook across the camp in frustration. 'I lied, ok? I didn't want to freak you out, but last night, I heard footsteps around the camp. I thought it was an animal, a fox or a really big dog or something but this morning, I found this.' Stalking across the camp with Jen following at his heels, Landon moved some leaves. Jen swallowed a scream as she looked at the perfect outline of a human foot. She quickly looked around to see if there were more but she couldn't see any. From the direction of the footprint, it was obvious the person had been walking into the camp.

'Who could it be?' she whimpered.

'I don't know. But Jen, we're not alone up here and I've seen enough horror stories to know when the heroes should be running. I think we should pack up. We've got some data. We can come back later in the summer. Bring more people, perhaps a couple of guard dogs but I really don't think it's safe for us up here,' urged Landon.

'Ok,' said Jen quietly. They both moved towards their tents and grabbed their rucksacks, stuffing whatever belongings they could into them. 'Do you think we'll be down the mountain by nightfall?' Jen called from her tent.

'I'm not sure. It seems to be getting dark pretty quickly,' replied Landon. Jen heard him zipping his backpack.

'Hey, I don't care if I have to walk out of here with only my lighter to help, we're leaving,' said Jen as she finished packing. 'What should we do with the tents?'

Landon shook his head. 'They're trashed. I say we leave them. It's the rest of the equipment we need to take back or the uni will have our asses.'

Jen looked up, through the trees. 'You were right about the daylight. I can't believe how quickly the sun's going down. We need to hurry.'

Landon didn't reply, but hastily snatched the upturned

cases and carefully placed the damaged equipment inside. 'Shit, they are going to be so pissed. I think the magnetometer is wrecked.'

'Are you sure?' Jen asked as she snapped her camera case closed.

Landon gave her a small grin, despite his stress. He picked up the magnetometer and shook it gently, 'Yeah, it rattles now.'

Jen struggled not to smile before a giggle erupted from her.

'You think your ancient people did this?' asked Landon.

The sound of a twig snapping hastened their packing. Jen rushed to Landon's side and he wrapped an arm around her protectively, holding the magnetometer in front of him like a weapon.

'What was that?' whispered Jen.

'Forget about the equipment. I don't care if they fire us. We're leaving now,' muttered Landon.

'I'm not leaving without my data,' replied Jen, grabbing her small backpack off the ground. She threw her camera bag to Landon who caught it easily before taking her hand. They both started running through the trees, uphill, towards the stone circle.

'Can you remember the way?' Landon called, struggling for breath.

Huffing behind him, Jen replied, 'We get to the stones, then turn right. There's a narrow path through the trees then it opens out and it's all downhill back to the car park. Please tell me you didn't leave the car keys at the camp.'

Landon let go of her hand and quickly checked his pockets as they continued running. 'Fuck!' he exclaimed. 'They were in my backpack.'

Landon stopped abruptly, Jen smacking into his back. 'Shit,' she muttered.

Landon turned to face her. 'I've got to go back for the keys,' he said.

'Don't be stupid. We don't know what's back there. Let's just go. We can hitch-hike out of the car park. Shit, I don't care if we have to walk all the way back to town but I'm not going back to the camp.'

Landon looked around them. The trees seemed to absorb any available light and formed strange shapes which played with his mind. He pointed, 'Look, there's the stone circle. Go there and wait for me. I'll be two minutes I promise, then we'll be out of here.'

Jen shook her head, holding on to Landon's arm. 'Please Landon, let's just go. We can come back for your car.'

Landon carefully detached Jen's grip, 'I'll be two minutes, I promise,' he said before disappearing into the woods. Jen watched as his pale t-shirt was swallowed by the trees then slowly turned and walked into the clearing with the stone circle. Not wanting to stand too close to the trees for fear of whatever had attacked their camp, she walked into the clearing feeling very exposed. She turned slowly, feeling eyes on her. Not really knowing what to do, she sat on one of the stones of the stone circle, pulling her knees up to her chin and wrapping her arms around her. The cooling air brought goose-bumps to her skin so she shrugged off her backpack and pulled out her jumper.

'Come on Landon,' she muttered as she zipped the jumper up under her chin. There was a rustle in the bushes. Jen focussed her attention on the noise. 'Landon?' she called hopefully but there was no response. Another noise, this time rocks tapping made Jen spin around, looking into the stone circle but she still couldn't see what or who was making the noises. 'Damn it Landon, we could have been half-way down the mountain by now,' she muttered as she turned back to he path Landon had taken.

Standing in the path to the camp was a tall figure, glowing white. Jen blinked and when she opened her eyes, the figure was right in front of her. She screamed as the figure grinned a predatory smile. Jen tried to push herself backwards, off the stone but slipped on the moss. Her back slammed on the edge of the stone as she fell into the stone circle. The last of the sun was swallowed by darkness but as Jen lay looking around her, she could see shapes forming out of the darkness, starting as small smudges of light before growing larger. The figure that had been in front of Jen glided through the stones. As he did so, his features seemed to form and grow clearer. Jen could now see that under the long flowing cloak he wore a loose tunic, cinched at the waist by a wide belt and hanging from it was a long sword. His feet were bare and Jen knew he was the man who had been in their camp. Struggling to remember to breathe she slowly raised her eyes to his face. His face was long, his features narrow but vaguely human. His lips were curled back in a snarl and his oval eyes were raised at the outer edges. He didn't have much of a nose, just two slits above his mouth which flared open as he breathed. He stepped towards Jen as she lay blinking, looking up at him from the ground.

'Who, who are you?' she whispered.

The creature didn't say anything but stepped closer. Jen tried to shuffle back but he leaned down and grabbed her by her throat, raising her up so her feet were dangling off of the ground and she was looking him in the eye.

He pulled her towards him as Jen shook her head, 'Please let me go,' she whined. Jen struggled against the creature, but his grip remained firm. Jen tried to push against the creature but nothing moved him. Tears streamed from her eyes as his mouth met hers, his sharp teeth biting the skin around her mouth. Jen struggled to breathe as the creature sucked the air from her lungs.

Jen was started to feel light headed. Her vision clouded so for a moment the creature doubled and shimmered. She knew she was about to lose consciousness and that she would die but she didn't have time to feel sorrow or pain. Her vision darkened.

'Brother!' a voice boomed across the clearing.

The creature pulled his face away from Jen's, little drops of blood hanging from his teeth. His grip loosened and Jen sucked grateful air into her lungs, her eyelids flickering open. Across the stone circle another of the glowing creatures was forming, He looked similar to the creature holding Jen, although about half a head shorter. The creature holding Jen snarled and threw her away like a discarded rag. She fell heavily, landing on her left shoulder. She tried to sit up but her left arm wouldn't support her so she rolled onto her right side and slowly eased into a sitting position. She managed to push herself against one of the stones, the cool stone easing the throbbing in her back, arm and shoulder. Touching her mouth her hand came away bloody. Jen knew she had to get away from the creatures but she didn't have the energy to get up. In fact she felt about eighty years old.

'Brother!' the second creature said again, more sharply this time. 'What are you doing here? You know better than to desecrate this place. You have been banished. The fairy folk no longer recognise you as one of their kind. Leave this place.'

A slash of a grin formed on the first creature's face, 'Ho! The king has spoken. Look at you little brother, all grown up. You know, Orin, I've been drinking from the human. All her fear, her love, her very life is pumping through me right now. Still think you can take me, you pathetic usurper?'

Orin paused, looking from his brother to Jen and back again. 'She's a mere whelp. I doubt you absorbed even a tiny amount of power from her, Alston. I did not fear you when I beat you before, and I fear you not now. However, this time, I won't just banish you from this kingdom, I will bury you beneath it. Long have you been a thorn in my sole. You will no longer threaten my people or play your tricks on the humans.'

'All your talking, little brother. I have learned new tricks since our last meeting and this time, I will defeat you, then all this will be mine. And you,' Alston looked at the fairy folk watching them, 'I will kill your poor excuse of a king. Then you will accept me as your leader.' Alston's grin turned malevolent, 'And I have plans for you all. We will retake our land. Kill the pathetic humans. Destroy all who stand in our way.'

Orin shook his head sadly. 'Do you never learn brother, this is why father denied you. Your murderous desires will do us no good. We are safe for the moment, but if you attack the humans, they will come, with their technology and their weapons. You have seen the destruction they have brought upon themselves. I fear for what they might bring upon us.'

'You are weak, Orin. You are as weak as the humans. I will defeat them as easily as I defeat you,' spat Alston.

Orin drew his sword, his eyes narrowing as he looked at his brother.

'I warned you, brother. I have given you every chance and you have thrown it back at me. This is our final goodbye.'

Alston swaggered towards his brother, casually drawing his sword. 'I will enjoy teaching you a lesson, little brother,' he sneered.

Orin struck the first blow, aiming straight for Alston's heart. Alston blocked the blow, deflecting the sword wide, then slicing his own blade across Orin's stomach. Orin jumped high, arching over Alston's head. He landed with ease and immediately swung his sword at the back of Alston's head. Without turning, Alston blocked the blow with his sword.

'I have drunk the life nectar of the human, you fool. I have strength beyond your imagining,' Alston jeered.

Orin responded by kicking Alston in the back, sending his brother sprawling. Alston turned his fall into a roll, ducking out of Orin's way as his younger brother swiped at him. Alston flicked his sword upwards, catching Orin's chin. He grinned as blue blood started to dribble down his brother's throat.

Orin wiped the blood away, the wound already starting to close. Seeing Alston frown he said, 'You are not the only one to have learned new tricks brother. There is a dragon tree, the fruits of which I have eaten. My healing powers are great.'

Alston took a step back, suddenly uncertain. 'A dragon tree?' he asked.

'The songs our father once sang were true. It is here, in these woods. Set your weapon down Alston, and I will share the magic of the dragon tree with you. Together we will be great once more.'

Alston pondered his brother's words. He moved to put his sword on the floor. Orin smiled and moved towards Alston, his arms ready to embrace him. Suddenly Alston swiped his sword sideways, catching Orin's thigh.

Jen covered her her ears and closed her eyes, desperately trying to block out the sound of the battle. However, despite her best efforts, she could still hear the clash of steel and the muttered threats as the brothers fought. Peeking, Jen saw Alston stab at Orin, slicing his chest but the wound began to close as Orin slashed at Alston, forcing him backwards, towards Jen. Jen shuffled backwards, looking for something to hide behind but finding nothing.

The battle continued, back and forth across the clearing. Alston would appear to take the upper hand, but Orin's wounds would begin to heal, the healing powers of the dragon tree rejuvenating him for another attack. Soon Alston was staggering under the blows from his brother, streaks of blood stinging his eyes and matting his hair. However, his hatred drove him on as he swung his blade once more at Orin.

Orin's blade caught Alston's, stopping it from cutting him more deeply. He kicked his brother in the chest, sending Alston flying backwards. Before he could stand up, Orin stood over him, his blade at his brother's throat. Alston glared up at him, the cut above his eye blinding him. Blinking away he blood he spat, 'Do it. Go on. Kill me.'

Orin's sword did not waver. 'I will give you one final chance, Alston. Begone from here, forever. There are plenty of glens that would offer you a home but do not return here.'

Alston sneered at his brother. 'I'm the true heir, Orin. We know it and so do our people. I will crush you.'

Orin looked at his brother for a minute, his gaze as unwavering as his sword. 'You have always been a fool, big brother,' he said quietly. Alston opened his mouth to respond but Orin pushed down on his sword, slicing through Alston's neck and plunging the sword deep into the ground below. Alston's eyes widened momentarily before the numbness of death froze them.

'I am sorry brother,' whispered Orin. He pulled his sword from his brother's throat with a sucking sound. Jen struggled not to scream and pushed herself further against the stone behind her. The sound made Orin turn to her and she shrieked.

The king gave her a small smile. 'Do not fear, human. I will not harm you. You have experienced much in your time here, but the sun is setting on us and you must return to your home.'

'How do I do that?' asked Jen in a tiny voice.

Orin's smile broadened. Jen flinched as he lifted his arm. 'Exactly how you entered my kingdom, simply step out of the circle. I am sorry our hospitality has not matched that of my ancestors, but I am sure you can appreciate, I must mourn the passing of my brother. Until later, human.' Orin bowed his head to Jen as two of the fairy folk stepped passed him and picked Alston up under his arms, dragging his body across the circle. They slowly faded until Jen was left looking at an empty stone circle. The pale white light had faded and the haze of dawn was breaching the trees.

Sobbing, Jen climbed over the stones and out of the circle.

'Landon?' she shouted. Forgetting her pack, she tried to find the path to their camp but she must have got turned around because she couldn't find it. The trees seemed to be latching together to block her path. Finally; frustrated scared and crying, she found the path back to the car park. 'You had better be waiting for me in the car,' Jen thought as she ran down the path. The sun was round and bloated by the time she got to the car park. Looking around as she sucked the cool morning air into her lungs, Jen failed to see Landon's car.

'I'll bloody kill you when I see you,' growled Jen.

'Excuse me?' asked a young woman as she passed Jen. The woman was holding the hand of a small boy, approximately eight years old and she had a large rucksack on her back which bulged with similar camping equipment. The boy pulled at her hand anxiously.

'Come on, mum. I can't see Dad and Peter anymore. I

don't want them to start the camp without me,' whined the boy.

'Sorry,' muttered Jen. 'My friend was supposed to meet me here, but I can't see his car. I think the idiot must have left without me.'

The mother peered at Jen through thick glasses. 'Are you alright? You look awfully flushed. Do you need me to get someone to help you?' she asked suspiciously taking in Jen's ruffled clothes and the dried blood around her mouth.

'No, honestly, I'm fine. I just ran to try and catch my friend,' Jen cast her arm around the near deserted car park, 'and I still missed him. He's going to be in so much trouble when I catch up with him.'

'Well, I hope you find him. Ok, Carl, we're going now. We'll soon catch up to Dad and Peter and they can't set up the camp without us, calm down,' soothed the woman.

Jen opened her mouth to warn the woman against camping in the woods when she saw the local bus about to pull away from the visitors centre.

'Be careful,' she called after the woman and her son before focussing the last of her energy on catching the bus.

Jen's annoyance at Landon deserting her fuelled her anger all the way into town. Seeing the university campus, she rang the bell and was pushing her way off the bus before the doors had fully opened. She sprinted across the campus and her anger gave her extra bounce up the steps to the university until within minutes she was standing in front of Landon's office. She walked in without knocking.

Landon was sitting behind his desk, papers strewn everywhere, typing an email.

'Where the hell did you get to?' Jen yelled.

Landon spun, knocking his coffee mug across his desk. The cold dregs of coffee splashed over his notes and papers.

'I'm really sorry,' he said, standing and mopping the coffee spots, 'I wasn't aware I was due to be somewhere.'

'Due to be somewhere? Due to be somewhere?' Jen's voice rose. 'You were supposed to come and get me. You weren't supposed to desert me in the middle of fucking nowhere and then sit here and drink coffee!' Jen swiped the top layer of papers off of the desk and onto the floor.

Landon's head snapped up and for the first time he looked at Jen.

'Jen?' asked Landon, slipping his glasses off of his nose. 'Jen, is that you?'

'What the hell do you mean, is that you? Of course it's bloody me. What the hell were you thinking, leaving me at the stone circle last night? Anything could have happened. And actually, anything did. You won't believe what I saw, Landon. I mean, I was terrified, I thought Alston was going to kill me, but then the others arrived, there was fighting, and Orin said I could leave and there was something about a dragon tree. Landon, it's true. There is something special about that stone circle.'

'Jen, calm down. I don't understand any of this,' Landon said, raising his hands to try and get Jen to stop talking.

'What's there not to understand? I was right. There is something mystical about those stones. We have to go back. Now, I know the equipment we used last time didn't function that well and I've been thinking about that. I know it's hokum but what about dousing rods? I also think we need to take more soils for analysis. I think a small excavation, perhaps in the northern part of the circle, because that's where they seemed to come from, and then...'

'Jen please, shut up,' Landon said sharply. 'None of that is going to happen.'

Jen frowned at him, 'Why the hell not?' she demanded.

'You've been gone ten years. We all thought you were dead,' Landon shook his head incredulously.

Jen slumped into one of Landon's chairs, knocking more of his papers to the floor. 'What are you talking about?'

'That night, Jen. That night, I went back to the camp site. I found the car keys and then I went back to the stone circle but you weren't there. I looked for you but there was this noise, so I figured you had got scared and made a run for the car park and left me. So I ran down to the car but you weren't there. I waited. And I waited but you didn't come. Eventually I got really freaked out so I drove back to town to get help. The police were out with sniffer dogs, they even got one of the recovery helicopters out to look for you, but they had to return to base when the fog got too bad. The police said it's not uncommon for people to go missing in the woods, but that they nearly always turn up. Then when we couldn't find any trace of you, they started asking me questions. Even had me in custody for a while. Found your back pack by the stones but that was it. If there had been any other evidence I'd hurt you, I'd have been charged with your murder but as it was, they just thought we'd had an argument and you'd stormed off. I just can't believe you're here.'

'I don't understand. It's only been one night,' muttered Jen.

'Photos,' blurted Landon. He scrambled around his desk and pulled out a folder from the pile Jen had knocked off the chair. Pulling out the photographs, he spread them across the floor. Jen leaned forward and studied the photos.

'I still had the camera with me that night. In all the confusion, I kind of forgot about it. It wasn't until about a month after you disappeared that I remembered and got the film developed. Look.'

Jen studied the photos. She remembered taking them when they were assessing the site of the stone circle. There were close ups of the individual stones. She had angled the camera to get a clear view of the markings on the stones. There were also a few pictures of the woods and surrounding area, including one of Landon attempting to light the fire. Jen smiled at the memory. Then she came to the last set of photos, taken on the day she had disappeared. There was the panoramic shot of the site, showing the stone circle. And in the middle, almost like a flash of light or a spot on the film, were the shadowy images of the tall fairy folk.

The Cairn

She slowly came to wakefulness, the feeling starting in her toes before moving up to her knees, across her stomach and down both arms to her fingertips. There was a dull ache in her chest and a pounding in her temple. Gently turning her head, she felt the bones creak into place with reluctance before she stretched the rest of her limbs. Her mind was cloudy and while her body cried out at the exertions of the day before, she couldn't remember what she had undertaken to feel so drained. Perhaps she was finally succumbing to the horrid disease which had affected so many in her village, leaving children without mothers, wives without husbands and children like herself all alone.

Struggling not to panic, a dull voice in her brain reminded her that she was suffering none of the symptoms the others had. She tried to sit up, pulling at the loose sheet which covered her. Immediately her head cracked into something wooden. She flopped back down before trying to sit up again but with the same result: there was something hard above her. Had she managed to fall out of bed and roll under it in her sleep? Breathing through her nose to try and control her rising panic, her hands were momentarily caught in the rough linen sheet before they flew above her head, her knuckles smacking into the wooden slats. Splinters pressed into her skin, but not enough for them to break the surface. Her hands explored and she realised she was confined on all side. She shifted her body to try and ease the cramp forming in her calves but frowned when her movements were blocked. Her legs kicked out and she heard them tapping against wood. Spreading her fingers out, her hands stretched out, hitting the wooden slats above her. Feeling the rough wood, and the close slats, she realised she wasn't under her bed. Her fingers danced over the wood, revealing her confinement. she pushed against the top of the box: she couldn't bring herself to call it a coffin. Air breezed through the gaps in the slats but the top stayed resolutely in place.

Pounding the coffin in frustration, she tried to remember her name, her family, anything about where she had come from but all was met with an annoying blank. Slowly images filtered through her consciousness: she remembered her village, which was in the grip of some unknown plague, the families in their round houses, the priests screaming to their gods. Those affected had been left to die, their houses burning around them. The image of a young girl kept coming back to her: was it the face of her sister or daughter?

Her fingers moved to her eyes. She felt more of the rough wiry thread sewn through her eyelids, forcing her eyes closed. There was a moment of panic which she hastily swallowed: she needed to remain calm if she was going to get out of the coffin and find the person who had done this to her. Her fingers moved back and forth as she tried to locate the ends of the thread but at each end she came across thick knots. Pulling at them she felt no pain but equally, the knots refused to loosen. She debated what to do: pulling at the thread would tear her eyelids, but leaving them in place would mean she was blind. Raising her head to one of the breezes coming in through the slats, she couldn't distinguish between light and dark and so assumed that wherever she was, it was dark inside so being able to see would do her no good anyway.

She tried to open her mouth to scream for help but her lips stayed firmly together. Breathing rapidly through her nose, her hands flew to her face, feeling the wiry thread which criss-crossed her lips. Her dry tongue ran over the rough thread which bound her lips together. The thread pulled at her tongue as she eased her chapped fingers along her mouth, looking for an end. She pulled at the thread, tugged until an end came free and then she worked slowly to unwind it until her lips were free, her focus on her present task keeping her calm. As she pulled the last stitch free, her jaw fell open. Her body sucked air into her lungs automatically.

Now she was able to breathe through her mouth, she felt strangely calmer. She knew she was in a coffin but she didn't remember who had put her there. She didn't know what they wanted with her, or what they planned to do to her.

She didn't know if they would come back. They might come back! The thought spurred her into action. Her fingers flew across the rough wooden slates and she ignored the splinters which lodged in her skin and the rough edges which tore at her nails. The top refused to budged so she pushed experimentally at the wood by her head, bracing herself against the bottom board. Grunting in exertion she paused, before putting her hands against the corners of the coffin and pushing again. This time she felt a slight movement, not by her hands, but her feet. Kicking experimentally, one of the boards gave slightly, before easing back into place. Relief coursed through her: she would escape this hell and return to her village, then they would hunt whoever had done this to her.

She slammed her feet against the coffin. And again. She pounded the wood as tears fought to creep between her closed eyelids. She paused, then she hit the wood again, this time in a rhythm, listening. Something was coming back. She remembered a fire. And trees. She was in the woods near their settlement, collecting the bluebells which had started to bloom. And water, she could hear water. The lake was close by. She had never entered the woods, had always been told that there were dangerous creatures in there who would attack, who weren't of this world, who would steal her soul. But it wasn't unknown creatures that came out of the trees: it was men draped in long robes, their faces covered.

Her thoughts were interrupted as the wood at her feet finally splintered and broke. She kicked the rest of the panels until there was a gap large enough for her to squeeze through, then shuffled out of the coffin. She emerged, a child reborn, and stood, finding a strength she had never felt before. Raising her arms she felt cool stone on all sides: they had built a cairn, as if that could contain her now.

She stretched her body as slowly and painfully, her memories returned. The men had grabbed her. She remembered being forced to drink a foul smelling liquid which burned her nose and brought tears to her eyes. She had tried to stop, to vomit the noxious liquid but the men in long robes had stopped her, pulled her head back and poured the rest of the liquid down her throat as she tried desperately not to choke. By the time they released her, her head was spinning and she struggled to remain upright. One of the men held her up while the others circled around her: singing, swaying.

She couldn't make out what they were saying, but the continuous rhythm was making her drowsy. She stumbled but the hooded figure kept her standing. Through heavy lids she saw the silver glint but her brain didn't register it's meaning until the cold metal pierced her chest.

Sobbing, her fingers danced up her stomach, to her chest. They slowly encircled the blade still lodged there. She started to pull the blade from her chest when a new thought struck her.

She knew what she must do. An evil sickness plagued her village. She must return to her people for she was their sacrifice and now she must offer them thanks and answer their prayers.

The Swamp

The Mudd People of the Wild Woods are not born: they are made. They are created from the very land in which they live. If you would like to make your own mudd person, follow these easy steps. Now remember, the mud used cannot be any but only that collected from the Wild Woods, when the blue moon is at its highest. It can only be collected by the seventh daughter of the eighth son and must be placed in a bag containing silver lining spun from starlight.

Ingredients:
Mud collected from the Wild Woods. You will need about the size of a loaf.
Blood of the Dragon Tree. Collect by the light of the new moon and be sure to leave an offering to the Dragon.
Water from the lake, collected after the month of sacrifice.
Hair stolen from a werewolf.
Freshly picked bluebells to colour the eyes.

Method:
Once you have completed the purification ritual in the Book of Wytches and called the four quarters of the circle, you are ready to make your mudd baby.
First, lay out your ingredients. Timing is key and the whole baby will be lost if you delay any of the steps.
Mix the mud with thirteen drops of the lake water. Make sure you measure precisely or the mixture will be too wet or too dry: too wet and your baby will be floppy, too dry and it will crumble.
Massage gently and slowly begin to form into your chosen form for your mudd baby.
Once you are happy with the shape you have created, make a hole in the area the heart should be. It needn't be too wide but must be big enough to absorb three drops of the

blood of the Dragon Tree. Allow the first drop to be fully absorbed before the second and third. Carefully push some mud to cover the hole.

Now take the hair you stole from the werewolf and push it into the baby's head. Not too deep or it won't grow but far enough so it doesn't fall out.

Using your thumbs form two (or however many you would like) eyes. Dip the bell end of the blue bells into the lake water and then place with the open end face out. Do not push or the blue bells will be crushed and your baby will not be able to see. Do not worry, the lake water will keep them in place.

If you want your mudd baby to be able to speak, cut a small mouth using your nail. If not, move on to the next step.

Build a small cairn for your mudd baby and carefully place it inside on a bed of moss and fern. Leave it to grow for three nights after which time you can remove the stones and welcome your new mudd baby to the world.

Recently some of the mudd people have taken to adding accessories to their babies such as twigs for hands or pebbles for teeth. This is not something we would recommend because the outcomes are unknown.

The Lookout Point

'I think we have a problem,' said Robin, doing her best to ignore the blisters forming on her feet.

'You always say that Robin, then you fix it. No matter whatever it is, you say "I think we have a problem" then you do whatever is necessary to sort it. You're ready for anything. For you, the ever fair Robin, there are no problems too large or small that you cannot tackle.' Robin rolled her eyes as Edward gave her a flamboyant wink.

'Are we nearly there yet?' asked Billy, conscious of the slight whine in his tone.

'Not much further,' Edward replied.

Robin, pausing to allow Billy to catch up with her and Edward, rolled her eyes. 'You said that an hour ago and we're still hiking. I thought this camp site wasn't that far from the car park. I can't even see the car park from here, let alone the information kiosk. Where are we going, E?'

Edward smiled smoothly, his brown eyes twinkling mischievously. He pulled his red university t-shirt from his shorts and used the bottom of it to wipe the sweat from his face, showing off his impressively toned abs. This time it was Billy's turn to roll his eyes as he pulled out his water bottle while Robin pretended not to stare. She brushed her red hair out of her eyes and wiped mud from her bare legs, ignoring the dirt on her shorts and t-shirt. Dropping his t-shirt, Edward ran his hand through his hair, flexing his arms as he did so. Watching Edward's performance, Billy nearly choked on his water, Robin quickly patting him on the back until he stopped coughing.

'You ok?' asked Robin. Billy nodded that he was, handing her the water bottle for her to drink from.

Edward shook his head sadly, 'Billy, Billy, Billy. Do the ladies at the newspaper you're going to work for know of your little drinking problem?'

'Sod off you poser. If you'd have spent more time in class instead of the gym, you might have a job to go to instead of, sorry, what is it you're going to do again?' Billy asked sarcastically.

Edward stroked his muscled stomach and flexed his arms again, pulling poses like a weight lifter. 'Time well spent my friend. The ladies can't help but run their hands over these beauties. And you know full well, I'm researching a paper.'

Billy snorted, 'Researching it for who? You're not affiliated with any museum or university.'

Edward raised a cryptic eyebrow, 'When I'm finished, every university and museum in the world will be begging me to join them.'

'Well until then, Indiana Jones, think you can show us where we'll be camping tonight?' interrupted Robin. 'It's past four already and I want to set up camp before it gets dark.'

'After you m'lady,' Edward bowed dramatically as Robin strode past him. Moments later he was jostling playfully with Billy as they both jogged to catch up with her.

Later that evening they were sat around the small fire they had built, their tents forming a protective circle against the horrors of the dark which the primitive parts of their mind had allowed to grow and become more frightening.

Robin plucked at a melted marshmallow, which was slowly dripping. 'It's a shame we didn't make it to the camp site today. It sounded lovely from the description you gave, E: the lake and that beach. I had a week of tanning and trashy novels planned.'

Edward didn't open his eyes from where he was laid next to the fire. 'We'll get there tomorrow. It's a little off the beaten track. You'll love it, I swear. Used to go there with my folks when I was a kid.'

'I can't believe so many people dropped out of this trip,' said Billy, staring intently into the fire.

Robin gave a small shrug. 'Well who can blame them? Finish uni, get a job, that's the plan isn't it? And hearing the offers Steph and Blake got, wow. They are going to be rolling in money.'

'Yeah, working eighty hours a week for a boss who doesn't even remember your name. Great. Where do I sign up?' sneered Edward.

'And don't forget, it's Stephanie and Andrew now, not Steph and Blake,' corrected Billy.

Robin laughed, 'Of course, how could I forget? Entering the 'real' world where nicknames are forbidden. Just think E, you'll have to start using your full name again.'

'Not bloody likely. I sound like a reject from sodding Twilight. I was Edward Cummins long before that stupid woman and those dickhead vampires. I mean, vampires that sparkle?'

'So you're saying you're not an emo vampire who glows,' teased Billy.

'Jesus, if I was, please stake me now,' groaned Edward. 'Anyway, Billy, when are you going to grow up and start using your full name, William?'

'When I'm a published writer. I can't wait to see my by-line, William Conners,' Billy gestured with his hands, showing his name on an imaginary paper.

'Yes, I'm sure your mother and readership of one will be very proud,' Edward continued quickly before Billy could retort, 'And what about our delectable Ms Robin Weever? What are your plans now uni's over?'

'Well, I've sent my CV out to some of the larger pharmaceutical companies, and there's always the option of becoming a teacher. They're desperate for chemistry teachers apparently,' said Robin.

'Ah yes, the cultivation of the next generation, the development and nurturing of young minds. Is there anything more noble?' Edward ducked as the remains of a melted marshmallow narrowly missed his head.

'And what are you going to do? I mean, what job can you get with an Anthropology and Mythology degree anyway?' Robin asked, skewering another marshmallow and positioning it over the flames.

'You forget, there's my research,' Edward said cryptically, laying down again and closing his eyes.

Robin and Billy exchanged a look of amusement. 'And when do we hear exactly what it is you're researching, o wise one?' Billy kicked playfully at Edwards's feet, trying to get his attention.

'All in good time, my friends, all in good time,' Edward said, not opening his eyes.

The rest of the evening passed as the group remembered nights out with university friends, terrible lecturers and the stress of final exams. They shared the bottle of cheap whisky Edward had hidden in his bag and by the time the fire had nearly died out, they were all merrily drunk.

'I need to get to bed,' said Robin, getting unsteadily to her feet. 'If I get any more insect bites, I'm bound to have a reaction.'

'Got your epipens?' asked Billy. Robin nodded and waved goodnight.

Edward waved to her from his position on the ground by the fire, 'I hear it can be cold out here with only a sleeping bag between you and the elements. I could crawl inside and keep you warm?'

Robin shook her head, which caused her whole body to sway and she did a mini dance on the spot as she struggled to remain upright, 'I'll take my chances with the elements,' she said as she waved goodnight to the boys and unzipped her tent. A few minutes later Billy and Edward could hear her snoring. They struggled to contain their giggles.

'I can't believe you said that to her,' laughed Billy, handing the near empty bottle of whisky to Edward who was now looking thoughtfully at Robin's tent. He turned his attention to Billy as the other boy kept hitting his arm with the bottle. Snatching it from Billy, Edward took a long swig.

'She's always so prim and proper. God, she's almost like a nun,' growled Edward.

Billy laughed, 'Just around you, E.'

'You ever get a taste of that?' asked Edward, taking another swing of whisky before handing the bottle back to Billy.

'Nah, man,' Billy said wistfully.

Edward continued looking at her tent. 'Think she's a lesbian?' he asked.

Billy laughed loudly, the noise resonating in the silent woods, the trees bouncing the noise around, distorting it before sending it back towards the camp. 'No, E, Robin's not a lesbian. Just because she's not flinging her knickers at you, doesn't mean she prefers girls. Well, she might prefer girls to a night with you, but I think she's into guys. I still remember that night you pretended to get lost on your way to the loo and ended up in her room. I'm not sure who screamed louder: her when she saw you, or you when she kicked you out.'

'Never really saw her with anyone though. I mean, four years at uni and I can't remember her having a single one night stand or a drunken night's groping,' mused Edward.

Billy laughed again, 'Well, E mate, you did more than enough of that for all of us. I remember that first night in dorms and you were sneaking that girl you'd met at the takeaway into your room.'

Edward smiled at the memory, 'The delightful, damn it, what was her name? How could I have forgotten her?'

'So many takeaways, so little time,' grinned Billy. This time it was Edwards's turn to laugh.

When Robin emerged from her tent the next morning, she found the boys curled up next to each other, Billy hugging the empty whisky bottle and Edward's arm thrown over his friend's waist.

'Bloody hell, E, you really will shag anything won't you?' joked Robin as she nudged the boys awake. Edward woke with a snort while Billy groaned and rubbed his head.

'What the hell?' muttered Billy, looking around him with a dazed expression.

Edward rolled on his back and flung his arm over his eyes. 'Kill me. Please, be merciful, just kill me now,' he groaned.

Robin laughed at their obvious misery as she quickly piled twigs onto the fire, poured water from her bottle into the saucepan and pulled out the sausages from the cooler bag.

As soon as the water had boiled she handed each of the still groaning boys a cup of tea which steamed in the cool morning air, and soon the air was filled with the smell of crackling sausages. Catching the smell, Edwards's eyes snapped open and he launched himself upright, sprinting into the wood where the sound of vomiting could soon be heard. Robin grinned as Billy swallowed paracetamols with his tea.

'Quite a night,' she said, handing Billy a sausage in a bun. She tossed him the bottle of ketchup which he caught with difficulty.

'Hmm,' replied Billy, studying his sandwich intently.

'Eat it. It will help absorb the alcohol. And once our gallant leader returns, he can have one too. He needs to be on form today if he's going to get us to the lake. I can't wait to have a swim.' Billy continued staring at his sandwich while Robin noisily took a bite from hers.

Edward stumbled back into the campsite, wiping vomit from his chin.

'Forget killing me,' he muttered, 'I think I'm already dead. This has to be what death feels like.'

'I can't believe it would be this painful,' Billy said quietly, taking an experimental bite from his sandwich. He swallowed with care, and, reassured he wasn't going to start vomiting himself, he quickly finished it.

Robin watched the boys in amusement. 'Hey, E, I've cooked you some sausages. You want ketchup?' she asked, holding out the sandwich and bottle towards Edward.

The colour that had started to creep back into Edward's face drained again and Robin laughed as the pale-faced Edward sprinted back into the trees. She shrugged, 'Oh well, more for me.'

It took the group longer than expected to pack their tents and equipment and the sun was high in the sky by the time they started hiking again.

'Are you sure you're ok to be leading us, E? You can barely see the compass, let alone where we're going,' asked Robin.

'My darling Robin, regardless of the pain in my head, I have an innate sense of direction,' grinned Edward, wincing as the movement caused a sudden pain to shoot through his head.

'It's just that we seem to be heading deeper into the woods, and I don't know, I kind of thought we'd go downhill to the lake, rather than uphill towards the caves,' pushed Robin.

Billy took off his sunglasses and looked around him. 'She's got a point mate. I can't even see the sun anymore. Oh, shit. What's that hanging in the trees? Are those animals?'

Robin stood beside Billy and looked to where he was pointing. The blood drained from her face. 'Oh my god, I think you're right. Who would put animals in the tree like that?'

'Hunters?' ventured Billy, feeling the sausages he'd eaten earlier churning in his stomach.

'It looks like they've been skinned though,' whispered Robin. She turned to Edward, 'I really think we're going in the wrong direction, E. I think we should go back.'

Edward glared at both of them. 'I know exactly where we are headed. We are not lost. If you hurry up a bit, we will be there soon. Now come on!'

Robin and Billy looked at each other, their uncertainty and growing fear mirrored in the others face. Edward had always been so relaxed and easy-going. In fact neither could remember him speaking sharply or acting so angrily before. Taking each other's hand, they slowly followed Edward as he stalked up the hill.

Their unease increased as the trees grew denser. They saw more of the mutilated animals hanging from the trees. The ground became more uneven and they frequently tripped as weeds and roots snared their feet. Robin and Billy clung to each other, muttering and complaining quietly over twisted ankles. They called out to Edward frequently, asking if they were nearly there, or telling jokes, but soon their enthusiasm was gone and they walked in silence. Edward continued ahead of them and did not look back.

Robin tripped over a large root, landing heavily and crying out in pain. She spun over, flinging her bag beside her and clutching her wrist. She winced as pain shot up her arm. Billy rushed to her side, but she brushed him away, annoyed.

'Where the hell is he taking us? We're not heading for the campsite, I'm sure of it. Oi! E. Where the hell are we going?' shouted Robin, hugging her rapidly swelling wrist close to herself.

Edward was above them, standing at the top of the hill and they could only just make out his t-shirt through the thicket. 'We're nearly there, I promise. It's a surprise. Climb up here and you'll see. The views from the lookout are amazing,' he called back before his red t-shirt disappeared again.

Billy took Robin's good arm and carefully helped her up. She smiled her thanks. They both looked uncertainly up the hill where they had last seen Edward. Billy shrugged, 'At least at the top of the hill we should have a better view, perhaps try and see exactly where we are and plan how to get out. How's your arm?'

Robin's wrist had swollen and a purple bruise was spreading. However she was able to move it a little so no bones were broken. 'I'm going to kill him,' she said, not taking her eyes from the top of the hill. 'I'm going to walk up that hill and I'm going to literally kill him. Where the hell has he brought us? And what's with all the dead animals. I feel like a creep with a chainsaw is about to leap out and cut off our faces.'

Billy snorted, 'You watch too many horror movies.'

Robin smiled at him as Billy retrieved her bag from where she had thrown it. He waved her away as he loosened the straps and flung it over his shoulders. 'If this was a horror movie, who'd play you?' she asked. Robin accepted Billy's arm as they both struggled to climb the steep hill.

'Knowing my luck, I'd probably have someone like Matthew Lillard or that guy from Frasier, the brother, David Hyde Pierce.' Billy snagged a tree root and pulled himself up the slope. Securing himself, he turned and helped Robin. He noticed that she kept her injured wrist close to her body, wincing when she knocked it against a tree stump.

Grunting, she finally stood next to him. Looking at him she said, 'I don't know. I can see you being played by Jude

Law. Or perhaps one of the Hemsworth brothers. Here, can you give me a push?' Turning her back to him, Robin grabbed a tree root and prepared to be pushed higher.

A smile danced on Billy's lips for a moment, the concern crossed his face as he pondered exactly where to push Robin. His hands darted between her waist and bottom before he finally shrugged, cupped her bottom, and asked 'Ready?' before heaving her up the hill. Robin scrambled up the last part of the hill as Billy followed.

'Who'd you want to play you?' he called, focusing on where he was placing his feet. Edward and Robin had dislodged a lot of roots and the soil was now loose, making his progress slower than his friend's as he clung to the dirt. 'Would you want someone like Scarlet Johansson? Or perhaps Natalie Portman. In fact, now I think if it, you kinda look like Natalie Portman. Obviously the hair's different...' Billy's voice drifted off as he joined Robin at the top of the hill. 'What the...?'

'I have a feeling I'm going to be channelling Buffy before we get out of here,' murmured Robin as they both looked around the clearing.

Approximately the size and width of a swimming pool, the clearing was nearly a perfect circle. At its centre was a raised rectangular stone under a large tree. The splatters of red immediately told them what the stone had been used for and following their walk through the woods, they could tell the tree wasn't same as the other trees in the wood, with its branches which curled high up into the air and one oddly bare branch which almost looked like a serpent's head.

Billy started to walk across the clearing, but Robin grabbed his arm, stopping him. Stunned, he looked at her and she gestured to his feet. A row of red stones formed a strangely ominous circle around the clearing. Frowning, Billy bent down to investigate the red stones. He tentatively reached out to touch one but pulled his hand back as he realised what had turned the stones that particular shade of red. Long tufts of grass rose from the ground like spiky haired skulls, and pieces of bone were mixed with the rings of daisies like hundreds of miniature clocks.

'It's blood,' he whispered in horror.

Robin threaded her good hand through his. 'I think we have a problem,' she whispered.

One side of the lookout offered a perfect view of the whole forest as the earth seemed to drop away sharply, giving them an amazing view over the forest until the green merged with the blue of the sky. A few birds were gliding over the tree tops, the sounds of their calls bouncing around the forest, only to be answered by another set of birds. However, they couldn't see the visitors' car park, the information centre or any memorable landmarks. Nor could they see a path through the forest: the trees were too old, knotted together, and stood firmly in their way. Looking down, they saw that they would not be able to climb down the cliff face, even if Robin's wrist hadn't been injured, as it looked as if someone has sliced it with a knife, leaving a clean cut and no hand holds.

'Where the hell has he brought us?' Robin asked.

'I don't know, but I think we should find a way out as soon as possible. This place is freaking me out,' replied Billy.

'But which way?' Robin gestured out at the waves of trees blocking them from safety. They both knew which direction they needed to go in but neither wanted to admit it: they couldn't climb down the cliff face, nor did they want to go back the way they had come, through all the dead animals, which only left deeper into the woods on the far side of the look out.

Robin and Billy looked fearfully at the dead wood and naked branches forming faces, watching them. More animals were dripping from the branches, macabre tinsel. The trees were filled with the promise of pain and darkness.

'Shit,' muttered Robin.

Squeezing her hand, Billy asked, 'Ready?'

Robin nodded her head, every cell in her body screaming at her not to enter the stone circle. She took one last look over her shoulder as if to confirm to herself that there was no other way, and then they stepped into the circle.

There was no rush of air, no disappearance into another world or the appearance of mythical creatures. However, both Robin and Billy felt it, starting at their feet, then creeping up their legs, through their stomachs and into their chests: a tingling of evil.

Picking up their pace, they tripped as the grass grabbed at their legs. In fact, they only managed to remain upright by holding onto each other. Robin didn't know where to look; the ground was covered in pieces of torn flesh and bone causing her stomach to churn, but the thought of what might be waiting for them in the trees they were headed towards caused her to pause as her legs refused to carry her.

'Robin, are you ok?' Billy gave her arm an encouraging tug, as a rider would a horse to cross a river.

'I don't know if I can go in there, Billy,' Robin whispered, the sob rolling up from her stomach stealing her voice. The foreboding forest looked far away now they were in the stone circle. The blades of grass were catching her feet and her arm was throbbing. The nearer she and Billy got to the trees, the more her body was forcing her backwards, trying to keep her in the light.

They rounded the sacrificial altar and headed towards the trees. Billy tried not to look at the animal parts on the altar but Robin stared in wide-eyed horror.

'Oh God, Billy, look,' she pulled away from him. Stepping towards the altar, she tripped as the grassy hands grabbed her ankles.

Bracing herself against the altar, Robin shrieked when she saw the blood seeping through her fingers and over her hand. Billy waded to her side. The grass seemed to be growing longer, chaining them.

'Robin, are you alright?' he asked, wrapping his arms around her and pulling him to her. Robin sobbed, trying to wipe her hand on her shorts.

'We need to get out of here, Billy. And where's E? We can't leave without him. Where the hell is he?'

'Oh, Robin. I didn't know you cared.' Billy and Robin turned towards the voice. Edward emerged from the tree line, ignoring the blood that dripped down his naked torso.

'E! What the hell?' demanded Billy, starting to move away from the altar, Robin still in his arms.

'I told you about the research paper, Billy.'

'Research paper? E, we need to get out of here. There's sacrificed animals all over the place,' said Robin, wiping her face she started striding across the circle, Billy close behind.

'Robin, Billy stay right where you are,' commanded Edward. Without pause he stepped over the stones and strode to meet them. His arms outstretched; Edward guided them back towards the altar. Neither Robin or Billy noticed that the grass had stopped catching their feet when Edward was with them.

'We need to get out of here, E,' whispered Robin, trying to push Edward back towards the trees. Edward stood firm.

'Why would we get out of here, Robin, when everything we need is here?' replied Edward. 'This is the point of my research.'

Robin stopped pushing against Edward. Billy moved to her side.

'What exactly is your research?' asked Robin.

'It's a secret,' Edward said with a giggle.

'Secret? Are you kidding me, E? We are surrounded by bits of dead animals. We are lost in the forest and there's a psycho out there killing creatures. We might be next,' Billy pushed.

Edward giggled again. Soon he was doubled over, laughing.

Billy and Robin looked at each other. 'What's funny?' Billy asked cautiously.

E straightened. As he stood, he pulled out a long knife that was strapped to his calf. He held the knife high so the sun caught it.

'While I was researching my dissertation, I came across this local myth. There's been suggestions and stories about dragons and a magical dragon tree going back generations.'

'You can't be serious, E. There are no dragons, they don't exist,' said Robin.

'Are you so sure? I've followed the ritual as laid down by the first settlers here.' The knife flashed as Edward spoke.

Before Billy or Robin could respond, Edward lunged. His knife sliced across Billy's stomach, cutting deep. Robin spun to help Billy but Edward grabbed her arm, dragging her across to the altar. Pulling her injured arm, Edward trailed the knife around her forearm, a bloody river following his knife.

Blood fell onto the altar mingling with the animal blood sticking to the surface as Robin twisted her arm out of Edwards's grasp. Kneeling, she could see that around the cut across Billy's stomach a red puddle was forming. Billy's face was contorted in pain, sweat already dampening his brow.

Fear flooded Robin's face as she reached out to help her fallen friend. She carefully grabbed Billy and gently propped him against the tree near the alter before turning back to Edward. 'What have you done, E? What ritual have you been following?'

Edward grinned at her. It wasn't the grin she had become used to after four years of university pranks and drunken nights out. It was the grin of someone whose sanity had moved to a new location and not left a forwarding address. He carelessly twirled the knife around his fingers. Robin flinched back but Edward did not move to attack her again.

He leaned against the altar and absently brushed the knife through the blood, drawing symbols across the stone. Robin thought he had forgotten about her and Billy until he started talking in a low voice.

'I know you all thought I was crazy for studying mythology. I know you all mocked me, and not always behind my back. You thought I was lazy and a fool. If I'm honest, it probably was laziness that drew me to it. But I was researching my dissertation, looking at local myths and where they started, linking it with local literature and seeing how far a story would travel. One story kept coming up, not just around here, but I found a lot of sources from all over the country and I got thinking, what if it's true?'

'You're crazy, E. There's no such thing as dragons,' said Robin, cradling Billy's head in her lap. He had gone pale and his breathing was drawn and haggard.

Edward continued as if he hadn't heard her, 'So I looked deeper. I read more and I pulled all the pieces together. According to the legend, I need to make sacrifices over the course of a month, then on the night of the new moon it will be birthed. I've said the words, I've spilled the blood of the innocent, the virginal.'

Robin snorted, 'I hate to break it to you, E, but I'm not a virgin.'

Edward looked at Robin in confusion for a moment, then the crazed grin returned. 'Of course you're not. But he is,' Edward flicked the knife towards Billy whose blood was now mingling with the roots of the tree, draining down into the ground. Edward turned his back on Robin, their conversation at an end and he began muttering to himself, hints of half understood words drifting towards Robin.

'So what are you expecting...' Robin's voice trailed off as the earth around her started moving. The skull-grass retreated and small rocks began bouncing like water on a hot plate. The earth cracked, knocking over the altar. Edward continued his chanting. Steam coiled up from the widening split in the earth. A scream, half-eagle half-lion, pushed the rest of the earth apart.

'We're getting out of here,' Robin muttered, scooping Billy under the arms. He was barely alive and as Robin dragged him towards the edge of the circle she grimaced at the trail of blood they left.

'You'll want to see this,' called Edward, looking at them over his shoulder.

Robin paused, looking over to where the smoke was now pouring out in folds. The trunk of the tree had split, and Robin could see a reptilian head peering out as the bark from its branches peeled back to reveal scales. The head was followed by a long neck and a squat body, about the size of a people carrier. The dragon stood on six legs with its tail coiling around: the tail looked to be at least three times the length of its body. At its tip, Robin could see that the tail split into many smaller strands which the dragon seemed to flex as if stretching out its muscles. The dragon was black in colour although the wings which were tucked close to its back were a silvery grey. The dragon stretched its wings out, shaking them like a freshly born butterfly and Robin looked in amazement at the bright metallic red under its wings. The dragon completed its stretch with a yawn, flashing a bright blue tongue and long sharp teeth. The dragon shook itself and looked around the clearing.

Edward laughed in delight as he looked at the dragon and did a dance on the spot. The dragon cocked its head while watching Edward with one of its dark eyes. It blinked. Blinked again. Then it snapped its head out, snatching Edward and biting him nearly in half. Edward didn't even have time to scream as the dragon flipped its meal into the air, caught it and swallowed Edward in one go. All that was left of him was one of his walking shoes and the knife he had attacked his friends with, which dropped to the floor.

The dragon then noticed Robin and Billy. A low growl rumbled up its throat like a burp. Setting her lips, Robin continued dragging Billy back towards the tree line. The dragon bent its head to sniff the river of blood Billy had left in his wake. It snorted, then started moving towards them. The dragon looked like an ant as it scuttled across the clearing.

'Oh God, Billy I'm so sorry,' whispered Robin. Kissing Billy quickly on the cheek Robin gently laid him on the grass, grabbed her bag and ran into the woods.

Robin could hear the dragon as it crashed along behind her, trees uprooting in its wake. Robin desperately looked around for some sort of weapon. She experimentally picked up a log and hefted it but the aged wood disintegrated in her fingers. Robin was looking for a place to hide when an idea came to her. The dragon was getting closer as Robin hastily huddled under a small bush, praying there was enough leaf cover to hide her from the dragon. Ripping open her bag she emptied out its contents until she found her medical kit. The others had teased her about the full medical kit she had packed, telling her that the only thing she had forgotten was the sink. Remembering the playful jibes from Edward and Billy caused her to pause momentarily but then another tree crashed, forcing her into action.

Into a plastic food container Robin poured all her medication: the diarrhoea treatments, rehydration salts, lotions for skin complaints, pain medication, saline, antihistamines and codeine, emetics and even her solution of tea tree and citronella oil. Wishing she had a Bunsen burning to heat the mixture, Robin stirred the solution with a twig then split the packing on the clean needles which were in the medical kit and pulling back the plungers, filled each needle with the drug cocktail. Snatching her epipens she popped off their lids, then she waited.

She could hear the dragon sniffing the ground and guessed that its eyesight must be poor. It rumbled near her. Robin peeked through the leaves, watching it approach. Shrugging out of her blouse, she tied it around a branch, then keeping low she left her hiding place. Moving as quickly as she could Robin sneaked up behind the dragon. It was concentrating on sniffing her blouse. With a final inhalation, sucking in air as if it would give her courage, Robin jumped out of her hiding place, slamming all the needles into the dragon's side. The epipens immediately injected the dragon with adrenaline. Before Robin could hastily press the plungers on the other needles, sending a cocktail of drugs into the creature, the dragon's tail whipped close to her head, forcing her backwards, although the needles were still stuck in its side. The dragon whined in pain, a sound which was strangely human, before it turned to look at Robin. The dragon's tail whipped around, getting tangled in the trees as it tried to lodge the spikes into Robin. As the drugs began to take effect the dragon started retching, then scratching itself with its long claws. It pitifully flapped its wings, flashing the red undersides, before its legs were no longer able to support its weight and it slumped to the ground. Robin approached it cautiously, her eyes flicking between the dragon's head and its tail.

The dragon's head lay on the ground. As she drew close Robin could see the dragon's three nostrils twitching. She started to reach out a hand before pulling it back, suddenly uncertain. Waving at the dragon it did not move, and remembering her earlier belief that the dragon 'saw' using smell, she once more stretched out her hand. The dragon's skin was cool to the touch and rough like sandpaper. It stirred gently under her caress and its long blue tongue snaked out. Robin was about to pull away as the dragon's tongue twisted around her arm, tasting the blood from the cut Edward had given her. Robin grimaced at the sucking sound it made but before she could pull away the dragon's tongue slid back into its mouth. Robin moved to wipe the slime from her arm and was shocked when she saw that the cut was nearly healed, a silver scar the only evidence of the wound.

The dragon twitched, then lay still for a moment. Robin looked at the dragon, a mixture of anguish that she had killed such an incredible creature but relief she had not been eaten like Edward filled her.

'Shit, I'm sorry,' she whispered as she stroked the dragon's nose.

Remembering Billy, Robin quickly rose and retraced her path through the woods back to the look out. Luckily the dragon had cleared a wide path as it had chased her so Robin was able to follow the destruction easily. The horror of the clearing had not dimmed in the twilight: Edwards's lone shoe, the fallen altar, the bloody animal parts and the crater the dragon had caused dragging itself from the depths. Mindful that the sides could collapse Robin carefully looked into the hole but its dark depths revealed nothing to her. She kicked Edwards's shoe into the hole and waited to hear the noise as it landed. She waited a long time.

Picking up the knife she moved next to Billy, surprised to find him still breathing.

'Billy?' Robin asked.

Billy's eyelids popped open, then closed just as quickly. A

tiny frown of concentration, then he opened his eyes again and concentrated on focusing on Robin.

'Hi,' he croaked.

'How are you feeling?' asked Robin, feeling foolish before the words had left her lips.

'Last time I come to a party of E's,' joked Billy, managing to crack a small smile.

'Well, just think, you'll have a killer first story for when you start at the newspaper.'

'Queen of terrible puns,' muttered Billy. 'The dragon?'

'Dead. We're safe. Can you walk?' asked Robin. Billy raised an uncertain eyebrow but slowly nodded. Robin bent down and carefully wrapped Billy's arms around her neck, while she locked her own behind his back. She was just bracing her knees to lift Billy when there was a snap of a branch breaking in the forest. Robin and Billy froze, listening, but there were no other sounds. Robin moved to Billy when there was another snap followed by a loud crash.

'Um, Robin?' whispered Billy.

'I think we have a problem,' muttered Robin.

The Bluebell Wood

She asked have you ever been to the wood with the dancing bells?
He replied, my mum says that's the doorway to the seven hells.
She rolled her eyes.
Don't be daft, there's no such place. Come with me, I'll keep you safe.
Away she danced.
Into the woods they wandered in search of the flower,
in which his mother had placed so much power,
Past the dragon tree, its branches aflame,
Around the far side of the sacrificial lake,
The hunter and hunted playing their game.
On and on they walked so far,
In silence so their time together they did not mar
With feckless talk or promises untrue
Until they saw the sunrise of blue.
Do you hear it? She whispered and cocked her head.
I don't hear anything, he replied, it's as quiet as the dead.
She cried, We're getting near, we're nearly there.
We'll have so much fun, you'll have not a care.
Hurry now, come with me she begged, taking his hand
He flinched slightly at her coldness before the feel of her silken flesh warmed his heart
And he followed without thought.
Onwards they moved and finally he saw
The delicate blue flowers they had travelled so far for.
Can you hear them ringing? The music so pure She asked
He shook his head, their sound to me is masked
She kissed him slowly
She wanted to know, do you love me? Do you trust me?
He looked into her eyes, a swath of blue.
I'd do anything in the world, if it was for you
She smiled and caressed his cheek before
Dancing from his arms
She moved amongst the flowers.

Her long skirts were flapping, skipping over her bare feet,
her arms flung wide, a flower absorbing the midsummer heat
Can you hear them now, she sang and danced
And as he stood and watched her
The faint sound of bells began
Till they rang through his head and filled him with wonder
I hear them he cried
Tears streaming down his face
He ran through the bells of blue
Into her embrace.
However, she'd gone, disappeared from the site
And down fell the boy
Till he was surrounded by blue light.
Fear the bells, should you hear them
And ne'er do follow
Young maidens who beg you to take them to the hollow.
For death you will find
Chiming for you there
Amongst the bluebells.

The Teddy Bears' Picnic

'So 'ow's fings wiv you? Life treatin' you well?' asked Charlie, taking a heaped spoon of potato salad and dropping it onto his plate with a splat. A drop of mayonnaise dripped onto his hairy arm but he shook it off before grabbing a sausage and popping it on his plate beside the salad.

Izzy took a sip of her drink, the pink lemonade sending bubbles up her nose. 'Not too bad. Family's doing alright. Little Simon's started middle school last week. I went with him of course. Got a bit teary, cos he's growing up so quickly. He won't need me soon.'

Oscar patted her arm, 'They always need you, no matter how big they get: even when they've left the nest, you'll always be the first thing they think of when they have a bad day.'

'And just think, when they have children o'their own, you'll be drafted back in,' Zed said, a slight tilt to his voice as he raised a glass in toast to the idea. His family were originally from Scotland but had moved around a lot over the years. Little bits of him had been left in each place they moved: some would say a little piece of his heart, but mostly, it was his stuffing which remained.

'Course, they might just get rid of you,' grumbled Tatty, the large scar across his abdomen flashed, showing each of the poorly finished red stitches and one of his ears only staying on thanks to some determined strands of cotton. 'S'what happened to me. Got injured in a freak washing machine accident and my boy said he no longer loved me. Me ma stitched me up of course, but then it was off to the charity shop. Hell on earth it was, dumped in a bin with other veterans of the teddy game. Some rough characters there n'all. Luckily I escaped, came here. Won't never go back.'

'You're going to live in the forest forever?' asked Caramel incredulously, her downy fluff fluttering in the breeze. She kicked off the shoes her feet had been squeezed into and watched as the bejewelled plastic tumbled over the grass. The matching handbag was propped next to her plate on the table and contained a spare bow, some sunglasses which always fell off and a change of outfit.

Tatty shrugged, 'Don't see why not. No people, fairly peaceful out here. Could get used to it.'

Izzy looked at him wide-eyed, long pink and gold strands catching the light as she turned her head. 'But that would mean no stopping baby tears, no tea parties, no bed time snuggles. Tatty, you can't be serious.'

Tatty glared at the assembled teddy bears. 'S'easy for you lot, you've all kept your looks over the years, but me? Well, look at me! Who would love a teddy with a scar like mine? And I've nearly lost m'ear and half my stuffing got stuck in that damned machine so I lost a lot of weight. Trust me ladies, once your looks go, you're stuffed. And I don't mean with prime, machine whipped stuffing, I mean stuffed in a bin bag and sent to the dump.'

'Calm down, Tatty, you're scarin' the girls,' growled Charlie. 'I know you 'ad it rough, but not all bears get dumped. Look at Zed 'ere, been wiw 'is family, 'ow long it is now Zed?'

Zed opened his eyes and sat up from where he had been sunbathing, 'Hmm?'

Charlie rolled his eyes, 'I said, 'ow long you been wiw your family?'

Zed stuck up his paw, counting on his pad and thumb. 'Well, there was the old Mr Webber. He was a good man and I was his daddy's bear too. Then Mr Webber, he had a daughter who married Mr Cobb. Now, Mr Cobb, he'd never had a teddy and he never understood the special bond a'tween bear and bairn. Kept me in a box for a long while. Luckily when Mrs Cobb had her wee bairn I was taken out of retirement. And wee James? He loved me more'n his ma and pa. Kept me close, even made his grandpa drive down in the middle o' the night when he'd left me at their house: refused to sleep without me by his side. The most adorable babe. Even I shed a tear when he succumbed to that evil disease that killed so many babes. Then I passed to his little brother, a spoiled child who pulled my ears and who took after his pa in temperament. Wasn't a good time but finally he outgrew me. Never really got over the young master dying, and his brother was so awful. Didn't treat his parents well either when was their time but that was another story. Young Master Cobb became Old Mr Cobb and I never thought he'd marry, but he finally convinced a foolish young woman to wear his ring. In time she gave him a wee bairn but he was never a happy man. Many a night his wife clutched me to her as she cried herself to sleep, the bruises inside and out easy for all to see. The whole house was happy when Old Mr Cobb passed on, leaving Mrs Cobb and her bairn free of his tyranny. That's when they travelled down here and she married a youngish man, just as foolish as she. He's fairly harmless, the charming Simon but Mrs Cobb convinced him to buy a wee dog, and so between the babe and the mutt, I've suffered one or two injuries, but I'm happy enough.' Zed shifted and the other teddy bears could see where some of his stitches had come loose and his stuffing was showing.

Tatty waved his paw at Zed. 'See? See? This is what will become of all of you. For all the love they give, they also pull and tear and rip. Not worth the bother,' he huffed.

Caramel hugged herself, 'But there's nothing better than that first cuddle,' she grinned.

Tatty huffed again.

'We've all had our bad days, Tatty,' said Oscar, 'But we've always gone back to our families. It's what we do. I mean, look at Zed. He's half deaf and missing all his tummy stuffing. That'll be us one day if we stay too long in one place.'

Izzy decided to change the subject. 'Has anybody heard from Marshmallow? Her family moved and I don't know where?' A silence descended over the group. Izzy looked at each of the bears in turn. 'What? What happened? Where's Marshmallow?' she asked

The others shuffled uncomfortably and didn't make eye contact. Finally Charlie spoke, 'She's gone, Izzy. They decided not to take Marshmallow wiv 'em when they moved.'

Izzy shook her head in incomprehension, 'What did they

do? Put her in a charity shop? Donate her to some children's hospital?' she asked quietly.

Tatty took up the story. 'She got left behind in the house. They never bothered to return for her. Next set of owners never had no children and didn't want no teddies so to the dump she went.'

Izzy gasped, 'Not the dump,' she cried.

Oscar nodded while Caramel wiped away a tear.

Izzy looked at them through watery eyes, 'Are you sure? I mean, the dump, that's worse than having your stuffing pulled. And Marshmallow, she was always such a good teddy,' she whispered.

Tatty looked like he was going to speak but Charlie interrupted him, 'It's true, Izzy. We didn' want to believe it neither but I saw 'er on the front of one of them lorries the bin men drive. She's gone.'

The teddies sat in silence for a few moments, the only sound was Izzy's sobs. The lettuce wilted a little more under the baking sun and the mayonnaise in the potato salad began to curdle. The ice in the bucket melted, the water making the label on the bottle of wine floated to the surface like life rafts in some strange boating accident. Finally all the teddies managed to compose themselves.

Zed looked at them all before raising his cup, 'To Marshmallow,' he said. In unison they raised their glasses, toasting their fallen friend.

'So what do we do now?' asked Oscar.

'Well, we could follow Tatty's plan and live 'ere in the forest,' joked Charlie, only half serious.

Tatty looked thoughtful for a moment, 'Nah, I think you were right. Forest is no place for a teddy. I mean it's nice to meet up for a picnic once a year and all, but really? You guys had the right idea, I can't live here.'

'So you'll go back to your family?' asked Oscar, a hint of suspicion entering his voice.

Tatty shrugged. 'Think I might go on the road, see if I can't find another family. A better family.'

'S'right Tatty, that's a plan,' said Charlie, patting Tatty on the shoulder.

Tatty looked thoughtful for a moment. 'Course, I could always return to my family. Just pay 'em a little visit as it were. Just make sure they're alright.'

'But why would you want to do that, Tatty?' asked Caramel.

Tatty picked up the large knife they had used to cut the bread. He spun it around in his paw, watching the cold metal catch the sun, sending rainbow rays around the glade. 'No reason,' he muttered, 'No reason at all.'

'Tatty,' Oscar said, the warning in his voice clear.

Tatty held up his paws in a contrite manner. 'I never said I was gonna harm nobody. But you honestly tell me you never thought about it? Never thought about biting the family dog after that little bugger shook the stuffing out of you? Never thought of pulling the arm off the baby after they'd dragged you around the mud? And what about those families that just dump you in the attic to get eaten by the mice and rats? You honestly tell me you never thought of ways to get even?'

'But Tatty, that's not how we're made. We're made for love and hugs,' Caramel said.

'We're not all made for love and hugs,' murmured Tatty, the knife still spinning in his paw.

Charlie sighed in exasperation, 'Tatty, you're bein' ridiculous. You can't hurt humans. Zed, you've been round the block more'n most, you tell him.'

The aged teddy peeled open his eyes and looked at the young bears. He twitched his nose, as if the change in the atmosphere was something he could smell. Finally he tried to sit up, Oscar and Caramel rushing to his side to help.

He looked at each of the bears in turn before he spoke, his voice gravelly and crackly. 'I told you my story. I told you of the love I had for Mr Webber and his father. Then the dark time with Mr Cobb and his son. Mr Cobb the younger as an evil man and as I said, the whole house was happy when he died.'

Charlie's eyes narrowed in suspicion. 'How exactly did Mr Cobb die, Zed?' he asked, fearful of the answer.

Zed set his lips into a thin line. 'Now, I ain't proud of what I did, but it had to be done. That man was evil and he was going to turn his son evil too. I couldn't allow that sweet child to turn out like him.'

'What did you do?' whispered Izzy.

'I did what was needed. They say Mr Cobb died of natural causes but ain't nothing natural 'bout it. Teddy bears can be amazingly strong when they want and so one night, after the whole household had gone to bed, I climbed onto his bed, across the covers and onto his face, covered his mouth with my belly. Then I didn't climb off till he stopped breathing. Course, he fought me. It's where I got more than one of these injuries, nearly tore all my stitching clear apart but I couldn't allow that man to continue to draw breath. T'was best for all and I'd do it again if needed.'

Izzy placed a trembling hand over her muzzle while Charlie poured more wine for himself. Oscar held out his glass for Charlie to fill up as well and soon all except Tatty were knocking back drinks to help with the shock while Zed turned his face to the sun and appeared to go back to sleep.

'See?' hissed Tatty. 'S'not such a silly idea. And who would suspect us? I mean, we're just bears aren't we? Loved for a brief moment before being discarded without a second thought. Look what happened to Marshmallow. We need to act before the humans realise and get rid of us for good.'

Oscar looked at Tatty. 'It sounds as if you're planning a revolution, Tatty. We're not capable of that. We're just bears.'

'If old Zed here can kill off that horrid man, I say we can take on our stupid humans. Who's with me?' Tatty demanded, brandishing the knife.

'I don't know,' Caramel said slowly. 'I can see Tatty's point. Without the humans we could walk around as we pleased. We wouldn't need to hide in the woods once a year for a picnic. We could go out, live where we want, wear what we want. Not be stuffed into duffle bags or boxes. Not left to rot in the attic.'

'Not be sent to the dump,' finished Izzy. Caramel sat next to her friend and gave her a hug as Izzy sniffled.

'Exactly!' exclaimed Tatty. 'I say we take it all.'

'Now 'old on,' said Charlie, holding his hands up asking for calm. 'You've all gone nuts. The sun's gone to your 'eads. We ain't the type of bears who go and kill humans. That's not what we're stuffed with.'

Tatty's eyes narrowed. 'If you're not with us, Charlie, you're against us,' he growled. Before Charlie could move, Tatty had the knife at his neck. Charlie tried to move but Oscar was at his back, holding him in place.

'Oscar. Mate, whatcha doing? You've got a good family, ain't ya? Why would you want to hurt them? And you, Izzy, you were saying how much you loved your family before.'

Izzy shook her head. 'Tatty's right, Charlie. It won't be long before I'm sent to the rats in the attic or dumped in a box for the charity shop or worse,' Izzy's last words were bitten off by sobs. Caramel hugged her close and made soothing noises.

Charlie tried to turn his head to look at Oscar stood behind him, but the knife at his neck pulled at his stitches. 'Oscar. You can't tell me you agree with this. Your families always treated you good. Ain't you got your own spot on the shelf by the fire? That's nice ain't it? Why would you want to change that?'

Oscar looked for a moment between Tatty and Charlie. 'Truth be told Charlie, things haven't been too good on the home front. Her grandson's just started walking. Got a bit of a thing for me and loves to pull me off the shelf. Other day yanked me off and dropped me too close to the fire. My tail was smouldering before they noticed.' Oscar turned so they could all see the burnt stub of his tail. 'I mean, I am an expensive teddy and she's just leaving me to be played with by her grandson,' groaned Oscar. 'I can't allow that brat near me again.'

Tatty cut him off, 'You're with us, or you're against us. So which is it, Charlie-boy? ' he asked, tapping the knife against Charlie's neck.

Charlie glared at Tatty. 'I will never allow you to harm the humans,' he spat.

'Such a shame,' replied Tatty and in one swift move he sliced the knife across Charlie's neck, ripping all the stitches. Charlie looked shocked for a moment before the rest of his stitches started to rapidly unravel, revealing his milky white stuffing. A moment later and he was lying on the ground, his stuffing in bright contrast to the green-brown grass.

Tatty turned to the rest of the teddies, the knife still in his hand. He carefully blew off a small strand of Charlie's stuffing before giving them all a grin. 'Picnic's over. I think you all know what you have to do. I'll see you next year and I want a full report on how you've taken care of your families.'

If you go down to the woods today, you're sure for a big surprise,

For today's the day the teddy bears have their picnic.

But if you don't go down to the woods today and decide to stay home,

Check your bears for weapons before you go to sleep.

Back to the Campsite

An unnatural howl fills the tranquil night air causing birds to take fright so the flapping of wings acted as a backing to the surging howling. Suddenly the more terrestrial noise of terrified screams drowned out the howling. As quickly as it rose, all noises crashed into silence, leaving the night once more still and peaceful.

Today people laugh at the notion of a werewolf: man, the planet's supposedly most intelligent and accomplished mammal being turned into a feral beast all because the moon shines a little more brightly for three days a month. For generations people who believed themselves to be lycanthropes have been mocked, abused, outcast and more recently locked in mental institutions. It's now considered a mental or physical imbalance in which a patient believes they can transform into an uncontrollable animal and behave in a manner society deems incorrect. People visit their doctors to receive little mind-controlling pills and discuss their deepest, darkest desires and dreams with their psychiatrists.

Where's Freud when I have blood on my hands? And on my face? And on my legs and feet? Ok, restart, where's Freud when I'm covered in blood? Mental imbalance my ass.

My eyes sweep the ground around me, seeing every grain of dirt. There's a small whimper from the bloody mess of bone and shredded clothing at my feet and I absentmindedly kick what was once a man to silence him. He groans painfully, but the growl that bubbles over my lips stops him making further noise. I study his mis-shaped limbs and torn flesh with oozing wounds. Humans are such fragile creatures. The smell of his blood sent me into a frenzy but I'm calmer now and my other senses have kicked back into their heightened state as I study my whereabouts. I can see a caterpillar weaving a cocoon, its tiny pincers winding the silk with delicate moves, a bird on a branch above me ruffles its feathers to keep out the night cold, I feel the ground beneath me, moist with dew and fallen leaves and below that worms push through the ground in a never-ending feast. The smell of rotting leaves sticks to my nose as the man's blood flows into the earth.

It's on nights like this I am happy to be alive. However, the darkness won't last much longer and I need to find shelter before dawn. While the beast gets to play at night, the human walks the day. I need to retake my human form and find the cave I scouted out yesterday, possibly taking a dip in the lake as I go to wash off this sticky blood and the last of my wolf hair that gets stuck during the shedding process. Breathing slowly and forcing myself to not look at the still bright moon, I feel the change start to take me, my senses dulling slightly as the nucleus of my body shrinks. Hair flurries from my body like snow and my claws snap off, revealing human nails underneath as I flex my long fingers. My centre of gravity changes as my hip bone realigns with my femur. I shake my body as it continues to metamorphose into the creature I hide behind twenty-seven days out of thirty. Not much longer and I will look like a respectable member of society, albeit a blood-soaked and naked respectable member of society.

Werewolves are portrayed as tortured souls, doomed to fight the eternal battle with the untamed animal contained within. Such tales are told to help humans sleep at night. It's only by giving myself over to the animal inside me that I have survived so long.

That's part of the reason I like Britain - lots of small villages and isolated farms with plenty of open spaces for me to get lost in. People don't notice if farmers or the odd dog walker disappears. Smaller villages also have a lot of townies who own expensive weekend getaways. They're the best because they're not generally known to the locals and it's common not to see them for months at a time; so when they don't turn up for work on Monday, their colleagues just assume they stayed in the countryside for a few more days. Before anyone thinks to call the police, I've moved on. And Britain is also a nation of campers, like the man at my feet, people who like the outdoors and enjoy experiencing Mother Nature in all her glory with their family and friends. As if Mother Nature and her beasts are friends of man.

I tried the big cities for a while. They are so easy to get lost in, urban forests with tall buildings, trees of light and narrow streets leading to dead endings. The smell of the cities; car fumes, sweaty bodies crammed into too little space and rubbish all congealing together in an overwhelming stench that will not go away. My nose went into overload. Too much information pounding my brain, too hard to concentrate. Also, recent global events mean everyone is alert and suspicious of strangers, on the look out for anything that makes a person different or odd. Difficult to hide when once a month your body pulls, stretches and cracks into a different shape. Hard to conceal the beast inside when all it wants is to tear out the throat of the man blowing cigarette smoke in my face.

Better to be outside in the wilderness, where the air is pure and there are so many pleasing distractions but so few nosy neighbours.

I start to reach with my receding fingers for a final stroke of the blubbering pile of muscle and bone when I hear them coming.

Hunters.

Despite their clumsy attempts at stealth I hear them as clearly as if they were standing in front of me. They tread carefully, sticking to the damp leaves to absorb their footsteps and wearing fitted camouflage clothing in an attempt to blend in. They do all they can not to be heard, even controlling their breathing through their noses. But each of them rattles a little.

Teeth.

Like all serial killers they cannot resist taking a souvenir from their victim; they collect the canines from their kills and string them on necklaces which rattle in the silence of the night. It gives them away every time.

These hunters have been tracking me for a while now: nearly caught me in the last little town I'd hunkered down in. In fact they did catch most of the werewolves I had met there. Seems we'd all been drawn to the town's isolation in a sort of unplanned convention but someone had brought uninvited guests. I wasn't quick enough to get out of town before I heard the terrified howling. I vowed that night that I would not allow them to add my teeth to their sick prize.

I breathe in deeply through my nose and am reminded of the hunters, men who have become unwanted shadows following me. Their all-pervading stink floats on the evening breeze and my nose filters their distinctive scents. One had chips with brown sauce for lunch; a lover of greasy food I hear it congealing in his arteries. If I don't kill him, this hike might. Another of the men smokes, a disgusting habit which causes his every exhalation to flash like a beacon, pinpointing his position for me. The third smells too new, too clean, like antibacterial hand wash and baby powder. There's always one who's obsessively clean while out in the dirt.

I know these killers so well, perhaps better than they know themselves because I understand what drives them: the anticipation of the kill. The thrill of the kill is great, feeling the flesh give to the tiniest of pressure then watching the first buds of red emerging like a spring flower while listening to the ocean roar of the pounding heartbeat. Gives me shivers just thinking about it. Yes, it's the anticipation that's the best part. Like Christmas, the excitement builds until you get to unwrap that one present you've been desperate for, peeling back the skin to reveal the juicy bits inside, then you're on a downer until next year when the excitement builds again. The excitement they feel tracking me, hunting me, is like all their Christmases come at once and should they actually catch me, I doubt they will be able to contain their pleasure but I know, no matter how many of my brethren they kill, they will be constantly driven to kill more.

Just like me.

I tell myself that they are not so different from me. They hunt, they kill, they play with their food. Man versus beast. Ultimately it's a battle for control: we all have the beast hidden within us fighting every cell to be allowed out, it just expresses itself in different ways in all of us.

I drag my mind away from thoughts of cool flesh and

warm blood. So there's three of them. There were four the last time we met. They have lost one. I hope he met a violent end. The smell of the clean one also does not send flashes of remembrance to my brain. Perhaps they lost two of their men in that forgotten village. Men without names, no background and no connection with each other. The only thing that links these men is the worrying smell of gun powder. From experience, I know each of them is carrying a high powered rifle, loaded with their own hand-made silver bullets. The silver won't kill me, although it will burn like hell and will slow me down, dulling my senses. No, each of those bullets is filled with foxglove, hemlock and yew, a mix of nature's most deadly poisons that would act like a heat-seeking missile heading straight to my every cell. Yet, even this wouldn't kill me immediately but it would bring me down long enough for them to stake me out on the ground and remove my teeth as the poison eats my cells from the inside out like acid. Then, and only if I'm lucky and they are feeling kind, they will cut my throat.

The first time I came across these hunters was when they came for me in the hospital. I still don't remember how I got there, but the doctors told me I'd been involved in a car accident and said I'd been mumbling something about a large dog in the road that I'd swerved to avoid, ending up crashing into a tree for my efforts. Stupidly not wearing a seatbelt, I flew through the windshield and landed about 100 metres away from the creaking wreckage of my car. The shock numbed my body and I knew I was dying. Still, despite being paralysed, I remember seeing the great dog looking at me. It gently licked the blood from my face as more frothed up from my lungs and as it pinched my hand between its giant jaws, I lost consciousness.

I woke up a few weeks later from a coma in the hospital, bruised and bandaged. The doctors told me I was lucky to be alive and patiently listed my various injuries. However, they could not explain the crescent shaped scar on my hand which refused to heal despite their efforts. However, the rest of my injuries were healing more rapidly than medical science could explain, and the doctors released me into the world amid much back-slapping at their own ability. It's ironic that while the doctors were celebrating the fact I was still breathing, those hunters were on their way to slice my body to pieces.

I replay our first encounter at the hospital over in my mind. Like a puppy I didn't understand why these men didn't want to play with me, although they did try and toy with me, urging me to fall into their traps while they hissed like cats. But I have always been a quick learner and with my human ability to rationalise fused with my new wolf abilities and senses, I was able to spot their plan. I hadn't discovered the killer aspect of my wolf self and it would take many more moons before I relished the kill but I knew enough on that first changing to escape their bullets and poison.

I look at the bumpy scar on my hand. Not quite the kiss of life but it had the same effect. My fingers trace the bumps and craters of the moon. A crescent shape. The moon forms a crescent, twice a month. I throw my head back and look at the moon in her voluptuous glory. My transformation to human form stops and with her light shining on me, I feel the familiar pull along my spine as my limbs once more elongate, my nails become needle-point claws, my faun hair sprouts and covers my nudity and my teeth, well they become a weapon of great beauty. I stand at over two and a half metres tall and I feel that if I reach out, I will touch the moon herself. My wolf eyes can see her every crater; like wrinkles they belie her age and wisdom. Many a night I have sat transfixed and studied her every dimple. She is my master and I change on her command, live my life at her whim and do my all to serve her. I am her child. A moon child.

A wolf child.

A cracking twig and hushed expletive brings me back to the wild woods. The hunters are closing in but I don't move. Ignoring the smell of the drying blood on me, I breathe deeply again. The gunpowder smell is now mixed with the smell of nervous sweat. Despite their experience they do not possess the cocky self assurance of many hunters I have encountered. I sniff again; one of them smells different and it causes me to pause. Humans sweat when they are nervous: first date, work presentations, when faced with killer animals. They also sweat when they work out. Now, these hunters have been tracking me for a while and I've taken them over rough terrain but they are fit despite the chip-eating hunter's bad diet, so while they don't smell that fresh, it's not the sweat of exertion I smell. I furrow my brow in concentration as the air is sucked through my T-shaped nostrils and the separate scents send electric snaps to my brain, triggering memories. That's it. Humans also sweat when they get excited. A rookie mistake, it must be his first night out. The others are right to be nervous.

We are all creatures of the moon, those that prowl the night, and the annoyed snort of a badger tells me that the hunters have frightened their meal away. An owl glides silently overhead and the clicks of its beak indicates it's spotted the other predators who are stalking through the dark. The hunters dismiss the forest noises as background chatter they don't understand but I drink in these sounds, the creatures of forest becoming my private monitor tracing their every step. Another bonus of living amid Mother Nature. The predators of the cities do not feel the kinship of forest creatures and would not warn me like my forest family.

A snuffle at my feet tells me he's nearly awake. About time too. I know I roughed him up plenty, but I made sure I bit him before I drew first blood. That way his terrified little heart would have pumped the werewolf infection into his cells before my claws found purchase. Most of his wounds have meshed and he should have been up hours ago. Typical man, sleeping when there's work to be done.

I sit back on my haunches and watch him with my head cocked to one side, my ears flicking as they monitor the approach of the hunters. The wedding ring on his crushed finger tells me that he's a family man and his stained shirt suggests children. He finally opens his eyes and views the world as it truly is for the first time. Rolling over he spies me studying him and I pull back my thick lips to reveal my teeth in a wolf version of a smile. Before his brain can trigger a paranoid scream, my still-growing fingers clamp his mouth shut. His eyes widen slightly as my claws dig in a little, but the tug at the corner of his lips tells me he likes the pain.

Slowly climbing to his feet he stretches new muscles and cracks bones into place. I remember the pain of my first changing, fear of the unknown as an unseen force caused my body to move in ways I didn't know it could and take on a shape that felt wrong yet completely natural at the same time. My eyes opened to a bright new world, too bright with hospital lights burning like an unnatural sun and the sounds of electrical equipment, human suffering and muted conversation, smells of disinfectant, chemicals and poor food. My ears could hear the suffering of the people in the beds close to me and the muffled conversations between doctors and families. Even though it was the full moon when I awoke, the wolf had filled my very core and so even in my human state, I had all the heightened senses. Quite a shock when you can't remember your name, where you're from or even where you are. Even the sedative the nurse gave me to calm me down did little as the werewolf pushed any unnatural invader from my body with all speed. I envy the man in front of me and how he has awakened as a child of the moon, here in the womb of nature.

Adjusting to his night vision he slowly surveys the destruction around us: the flesh of tents hanging from boney poles, discarded plates and food, high tech equipment crushed, toys and more. Frowning slightly at the realisation he no longer needs all these objects, remnants to his past life he studies them as if they were unknown items and I know from my own experience he is questioning why he would ever need this stuff when all he needs to survive are the tools and skills all children of the moon possess. Jumping silently on the spot, he clicks his neck and loosens his limbs. As he flexes, he feels his new strength in every part of his body.

The hunters snap another twig and the noise draws a whimper from the pup. He looks to me for reassurance: the bitch who birthed him into this new world. My answering growl acts as reassurance to him. Like I said, in his previous life, this pup was a family man and like every good British father, he took his family for a camping holiday, no doubt promising his two pre-teens horror stories around the campfire as the wife toasted marshmallows. Bet none of them expected their horror stories to come to life.

As the hunters enter the clearing I growl deeply as the smoker sneers in recognition. The rookie stares in wide-eyed horror and I enjoy the change in his scent from excitement to fear as I click my claws. Obviously he didn't believe the briefing notes and I hear the small burp as he suppresses the need to vomit. His two colleagues ignore him, all their mediocre senses directed at me as they try to ignore the destruction of the camp site. While they may travel in a group, they don't work as one. Another mistake.

Like any puppy, he is finding it hard to focus his attention, especially when there are so many distractions in the forest. One second he is looking at the hunters, the next he studies the insects eating in the trees. However when a set of faces, familiar despite their wolverine features, appears behind the hunters, he yips happily. An adult and two pups, play fighting each other but who stop and focus their attention on the hunters as soon as their scent hits their small nostrils.

One things humans always forget when they tell their tales: Wolves always hunt with their family.

Made in the USA
Charleston, SC
09 May 2014